## *Praise for Gisela Heffes*

"Heffes's striking work brings the reader deep into her protagonist's dark and roving imagination." —*Publishers Weekly*

"[*Ischia*] asks us to consider the role that our own storytelling, and our own fantasies, play in our lives." —Greg Walkin, *Literal Magazine*

"... deliberately digressive and often feverish novel ..." —*Kirkus Reviews*

"Gisela Heffes's work has been paramount in building bridges between ecocriticism and literary, artistic and scholarly responses to the rise of neo-extractivism, which rethink the agency of more-than-human existents and environmental justice. As the modern world-system's first colonial margin, the region is host to a rich aesthetic and political archive of mourning and resurgence; *Visualizing Loss in Latin America* mobilizes it masterfully for a bio-ecocritical re-assessment of our planetary present."

—Jens Andermann, Professor of Spanish and Portuguese, New York University

### *Praise for Crocodiles at Night*

"A valuable, attractive, and interesting novel." —Ana María Shua

"Recounting the death of a parent is by no means a new theme in literature. What is new is not only how it is told, or perhaps the reasons that led to the departure of that loved one, but the author's expressive ability to convey the loss and the circumstances that occur once the parent is gone. That is exactly what *Crocodiles at Night* by Gisela Heffes does: the reader can look in the mirror of pain, see his or her own emotions reflected in the pages of a novel that tells the story of an essential loss." —Rose Mary Salum

## OTHER BOOKS BY GISELA HEFFES

*Ischia*

*Visualizing Loss in Latin America: Biopolitics, Waste, and the Urban Environment*

*The Mobile Zero of Its Mouth*

*Sophie La Belle and the Miniature Cities*

GISELA
HEFFES

# Crocodiles at Night

Translated by Grady C. Wray

DEEP VELLUM PUBLISHING
DALLAS, TEXAS

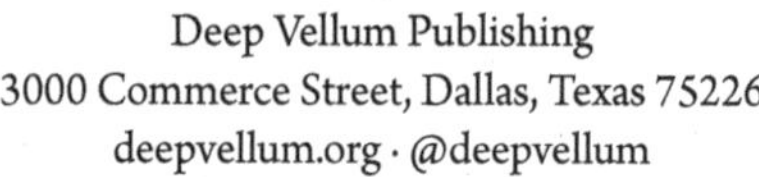

Deep Vellum Publishing
3000 Commerce Street, Dallas, Texas 75226
deepvellum.org · @deepvellum

Deep Vellum is a 501c3 nonprofit literary arts organization founded in 2013 with the mission to bring the world into conversation through literature.


First edition in Spanish as *Cocodrilos en la noche* by RIL Editores, Santiago de Chile, 2020. Second edition in Spanish as *Cocodrilos en la noche* by Editorial Planeta Colombiana S.A., 2023.

First English edition, 2025


Support for this publication has been provided in part by grants from the National Endowment for the Arts, the Texas Commission on the Arts, the City of Dallas Office of Arts and Culture, the Communities Foundation of Texas, and the Addy Foundation.

LIBRARY OF CONGRESS CATALOGING-IN-PUBLICATION DATA

Names: Heffes, Gisela, 1971- author. | Wray, Grady C., translator.
Title: Crocodiles at night / Gisela Heffes ; translated by Grady C. Wray.
Other titles: Cocodrilos en la noche. English
Description: Dallas, Texas : Deep Vellum Publishing, 2025.
Identifiers: LCCN 2024048282 (print) | LCCN 2024048283 (ebook) | ISBN 9781646053766 (trade paperback) | ISBN 9781646053896 (ebook)
Subjects: LCGFT: Novels.
Classification: LCC PQ7798.418.E35 C6313 2025 (print) | LCC PQ7798.418.
E35
(ebook) | DDC 863/.7--dc23/eng/20241118
LC record available at https://lccn.loc.gov/2024048282
LC ebook record available at https://lccn.loc.gov/2024048283

Exterior art and design by Jen Blair
Interior layout and typesetting by KGT

PRINTED IN CANADA

*In memoriam*

*For my father,*
*an unresolved matter*

*Hay golpes en la vida, tan fuertes . . . ¡Yo no sé!*
César Vallejo

*There are blows in life, so powerful . . . I don't know!*
César Vallejo trans. Clayton Eshleman

*Renunciar es acercarse*
*Cambiar nombres, apellidos, ocupaciones*
*Jerarquías, roles, ideas, costumbres*
*Renegar como ellos renegaron*
*Acercarse a los predecesores . . .*

*¿De qué estamos hechos?*
*¿Cuál es nuestra materia?*
GG

*Letting go means getting closer*
*Changing names, jobs*
*Hierarchies, roles, ideas, traditions*
*Denying like they denied*
*Getting closer to those who came before . . .*

*What are we made of?*
*What is our substance?*
GG trans. GCW

# CONTENTS

# (There)

Dad died today. It was foretold, but I didn't see it coming. I couldn't predict it. I couldn't guess the day of his departure. It took me by surprise, at Disney World. I'm not an oracle. I was on one of those trams in Tomorrowland, with my father-in-law and my two kids. Pushed along the rails in one of those cars that go from one future to another, speakers blaring about adventures, challenges, and innovations, I got the call. My brother called me from the Barajas airport in Madrid. He had just boarded the plane. Disney World, the world where dreams come true. He didn't see it coming. Neither did I.

What about nightmares? What would Mr. Disney say about nightmares?

*Notebook*

Let's pretend this story's main character does not depart from Houston's Bush Intercontinental Airport, but rather Orlando's International Airport. The airline she's flying is not United (previously Continental), but American Airlines. The main character of this novel is not Gisela, but Vera. Her last name is not Guerenstein, but Heffes. Vera Heffes. But let's also pretend they both have something in common: a father who is about to go into surgery.

# Day 1

Arrivals

Vera—or, rather, the plane that was carrying Vera—landed on Tuesday morning, five minutes before the plane that was carrying her brother, his wife, and their three kids. Vera saw the Air France plane land from her little oval-shaped window. She didn't see her brother, but she imagined him in his seat, looking out the window or down the aisle where the French-speaking flight attendants made sure everything was ready: seat backs in their full and upright positions, seat belts fastened, all carry-on items and suitcases stowed under the seat in front of them or in the overhead compartments. She imagined her brother thinking about her and her father, the father they shared and who was waiting at the hospital for his children to arrive and kiss him on his forehead.

*Notebook*

But perhaps the woman who got up from her seat and looked around at her former compatriots with a mixture of curiosity and strangeness was actually a third person. An invention, a hybrid, a new entity, a direct consequence of living outside the country for more than a decade.

This entity that we'll call Vera, but who could be Gisela, closed her yellow notebook and carefully returned it to her backpack. She would have wanted to write more. To describe the precise moment she got the call. To describe her reaction. To precisely write down how she imagined her father entering the hospital, the emergency room. The color of his skin. On his birthday.

Customs and Immigration

She didn't see the officer who was motioning for her to come forward. All her attention was focused on a five-year-old who was asking her mother to pick her up. Up, Mama, she kept repeating. A woman dressed as a police officer was almost yelling at Vera; it was her turn.

Vera had forgotten the brutal nature of her country's police.

*Notebook*

It was probably Gisela who went up to the booth, sad and suspicious, and explained the reason for her trip to the officer. Surely Vera would not have forgotten her mother's address, where she was going to stay, or her mother's phone number. Vera wouldn't have forgotten to charge her cell phone either. This not only happened to Gisela, but also to the hybrid she became, that person who began to talk a little slower than a porteña but who, despite the years she'd spent abroad, still had a notable foreign accent.

Exit

"He's afraid," was the first thing her brother said when he saw her. "It's a long operation." Her brother was almost completely bald. He had a bit of a tan, although it was the middle of winter and snowing where he lived.

Vera hugged her sister-in-law and kissed her nieces and nephew. They all left together and walked to a minivan that was waiting for them at the exit.

No one spoke as they rode along, or if they did, they spoke very little, as if time stood still. The highway imposed its usual uncertainty, but with that globalized-city glamour. Huge billboards bombarded their sight and other senses with imported brand-name products. Vera's nieces and nephew slipped in a word or two. At times they shut their eyes and rested their heads on each other's shoulders.

*Notebook*

She would have liked to have written a lot more. For example, to describe the scene where, when she entered the hospital room, she found her father lying in his bed. The silence or solemnity that surrounded him. He wasn't afraid. He was defeated. But she didn't know that then. She understood afterward, much later.

She probably stopped writing as she described his smile. How that smile turned into waiting and how that waiting injected him with fear. What might he have felt at that moment when his eyes met hers? She would have liked to have worked that out in her notebook.

The Hospital

The doctor entered with the usual arrogance. He asked the family members to wait outside. They all followed directions like obedient children.

The patient's family members were the daughter, the son, and the woman he'd lived with for the past twenty years: Lisa.

They all went down to the hospital coffee shop. The surgery could last up to six hours. Vera, her brother, and Lisa sat down at an elegant table that seemed out of place in a hospital. It was a solid wood table, square and modern. It would have looked better in a hotel, Lisa expressed. Vera's mother also arrived, although she had divorced Vera's father exactly twenty-four years earlier. Vera wasn't sure if she had come to be with them or to again step into the spotlight. She greeted everyone as if time hadn't coagulated. As if the rip she had tried to tear in the cloth had disappeared, and the time that had passed had suddenly become a seamless fabric waving in the wind.

When a nurse dressed in light-blue scrubs called their name, the family interrupted their conversation and looked up. They all stood, except for Vera's mother. She remained seated at the table, making up for lost time with friends and family members from the past who had come to be with her children and Lisa. Vera's mother didn't speak to Lisa's friends and family. Only to her children's friends and other old friends who, after the divorce and distribution of assets, remained on his side, her father's side.

Vera noted that her mother watched them as they walked away. They followed the nurse to the elevator. It was a different one, not the main elevator that visitors take to see patients. It was long and rectangular to accommodate gurneys. It was plainer, less elegant. There were scrapes on it, left by the friction of gurneys rubbing up against its walls. How many times had doctors and nurses, in a rush or in a critical emergency, pushed gurneys in or out of the elevator, convinced that such rapid movements would help save lives? *Save lives,* prolong that instance that many call life but what, for others, is pure agony. That moment when one is clinically alive, but inside—in that space that houses thoughts and feelings, senses, memories, quivering, grief, emotion—everything gets weaker and number until it becomes just an impulse, an engine without direction or compass, a rhythm lacking purpose. Something that's there even though you don't know it. Surely desires also weaken; they become precarious: exclusively supplying the most basic necessities. Survive. *Survive.* The nurse in the light-blue scrubs went with the family to the hallway where they would wait and talk with Dr. Casabilla. Vera noted that the hallway was between the operating room and the other wing of the hospital, where the patient rooms were. Vera heard a sound. Something like a scream. Then a strange silence that upset the family dynamic. Vera, her brother, and Lisa found a wall to lean on and wait for the much-anticipated doctor's report.

*Notebook*

She didn't want to write down that she saw his body, as stiff as a mannequin. His eyes open, empty; his hands raised and contorted like those of a paraplegic. She didn't want to write it down or think about it, but Lisa, without thinking, said it. She screamed in a sudden outburst. A dummy, a dummy! They've turned him into a dummy! She didn't want to put what had come over Lisa into words, and instead she hugged her very tight. She didn't let her see, even though Vera also had fallen into the abyss of that image. Her brother tried to soothe them both with an unnatural calm. Vera knew, and this she did write down, that a new image could erase an old one. You only needed to impose it, stand it up on pegs facing the other, the despicable one, and erase, undo, extract the other one away. She looked at Lisa. She grabbed her face and told her to do the same, to look deep inside for another face, other eyes, another look. To insert another image of her father that wasn't the image of a dummy and to eradicate the other image from her memory forever. Lisa looked through her phone and showed Vera another image. He was another person. He was smiling, had healthy skin, and was happy. His eyes were filled with light, and they had that strange and undefinable quality that floods us with life.

Post-Op

The image of her father coming out of the operating room had paralyzed her. She could not connect the person whom she had kissed on his jaundiced forehead in the afternoon with the body that was coming out now, completely motionless. She saw his eyes open, but they didn't see her. They didn't see her brother. They didn't see Lisa. They were open, but they didn't react. Dr. Casabilla came in, carrying a backpack where he must have carried his prestigious surgeon's uniform, or so Vera assumed. That uniform doctors wear to put on airs. Silent, like Lisa, paralyzed again, although not due to anesthesia, she closely followed her brother and sidled up to him. The operation was successful, was the first thing Dr. Casabilla said. Successful? They took out the whole pancreas. The whole thing? Was that necessary? He responded well to the surgery, positively. Is he asleep? Why doesn't he see us? Now we must wait. Why doesn't he see us, even with his eyes open? It's a long post-op. How long will he be in the hospital? You'll have to be patient. Will he be able to play tennis like before? Let me repeat: patience. Will he remember us when he sees us? He will be in intensive care. Will he live? If you have any questions, don't hesitate to contact my team. Team? Life expectancy? Six months? A year? Vera remembered that she had heard about someone who had lived for five years.

*Notebook*

In her notebook she wrote the following paragraph: I can't look at my father. I can't go into the ICU. I can't. I'm going to wait outside. I now have this new image installed in my memory like a microchip, and if I go in to see him, there will be another, a different one like that of the plastic dummy that's going to haunt me forever.

The ICU

Vera stays in the hallway. She waits without knowing what she's waiting for. She sits on a sofa in the waiting room right next to and facing the elevators that bring up visitors. There is a family of Orthodox Jews reading Psalms. That's what Vera should do, supposedly, read Psalms 74, 130, and 20. Pray for her father to get well soon, to leave the hospital, and to take a trip to visit her and her family. Maybe a trip to Miami. Her father loves Miami: strolling through the malls, speaking Spanish with Cubans, going to the beach. Maybe a short cruise. But her brother arrives, with her sister-in-law, and they let her know they're going in. No more than two people at a time, a nurse says. They're going in? Vera asks, without convincing herself that her fears are any different from theirs. Why is that? Why is it that fears are different, and what makes an impression on Vera is simply natural for her brother and sister-in-law? Her brother disappears behind a door with a buzzer and two small panes of glass. Behind him, her sister-in-law. Is she—Vera—a coward? Why did that image of her father stick in her head so strongly and not in her brother's? Or if it did, why was he able to get it out of his head so much faster than she was? She knew she had no other option. And she even felt ashamed that she had not been the first to go in to see her father. Haltingly, she went across the hallway between the waiting room and the entrance to the ICU. She had to grab ahold of the walls because she felt like they were moving. Or was it she who was spiraling? She grabbed the walls again. They got bigger and smaller. They shuddered like psychedelic shapes. It was all she could do to move forward. Everything around her was unsettled. When she identified her goal, she felt relieved. She rang the buzzer for the double doors and, once they opened, she gently slipped inside. She got close to her father's room and peeked around the door, but she couldn't see him. She finally went in. There were four patients in the room. All were men. This got her attention. The preponderance of men who get sick and end up in the care of others. A nurse cleaned one of their portable urinals. He was asleep. There were two patients on one side. Behind the curtain, there were two others. The dividing curtain on the left was open. The other side was closed. That's why she couldn't see him. A personalized medical team connected each patient to different monitors that measured heartbeats and blood pressure. Her father was at the back of the room, on the right side, near the outside window. The dividing curtain hid him. Vera could not see him even from inside the room. She drew a bit closer. No one seemed to note her presence. Her eyes followed her brother's and sister-in-law's shoes that remained motionless. The curtain didn't touch the floor. Regardless, she didn't dare. A rushed nurse accidentally pushed her toward the bed where her father was lying. She was diligently administering medications, emptying containers, and throwing hazardous waste like syringes and needles into the trash that was marked with a bold red biohazard symbol. Suddenly she remembered it was Tuesday. She had flown on Monday night. She arrived very early on Tuesday, around 8:50 AM. She hadn't slept on the plane. She had brought a yellow notebook and a pen to write. A long Tuesday, perhaps one of the longest Tuesdays in her life.

She took a deep breath and walked toward the bed. Toward her brother and her sister-in-law's feet and toward the hardworking hands of a nurse who was writing down numbers, volumes, and densities surprisingly fast. Suddenly Vera reacted. She couldn't enter the scene like that. She couldn't see, talk, and be with her father when her face was scared and wavering. She realized she needed to smile, to have a positive attitude. In the end, that's why she was there. That's why she had traveled thousands of miles. To be with her father and cheer him up. Not to be a coward behind a thick, rough curtain, but to hide her expression of fear and pain while facing a pair of eyes that looked at her with a certain naivete that Vera could never tell was real or pretend.

*Notebook*

That cowardly character named Vera, but at the same time Gisela, took note of her own movements and wrote down, perhaps with a sad irony, that with a bigger smile than usual I went over to the bed and said hi to my father. His eyes were closed. I looked at my brother and sister-in-law, interrogating them. Yes, he's awake. The nurse stepped into the conversation. He's under sedation, but he can hear you. My father nods. I grab his hand. I grab it firmly. I feel his strength in my hand as if this strength, this meeting of energy, established a kind of communication between us. I get closer and speak into his ear: I tell him that everything turned out okay and that soon he's going to get out of the hospital, and everything will be back to normal. He nods. I tell him my kids have sent drawings and they want to talk to him. My kids? When did I become a mother, and my father a grandfather? Am I not, perchance, the daughter, the girl, the tiny little one my father cares for and takes to school every morning? Am I not the one who needs to be kissed and cared for? The one who waits for a hug, a toy, or to be taken to a friend's house? I tell him that as soon as he can speak, I'll call my kids so they can talk. He nods again. His head is facing the ceiling, his eyes shut. I caress his forehead. His hand. Again, his forehead. It's my dad who is now lying there, flat on his back. My father. It's my dad who is lying in front of me, the same man who lived with me and filled my life and my memory for forty-three years. Only forty-three years, Dad. I want you to be in my life, in what I remember, in my memories, longer. Is that possible? Try a little harder, okay? Come on, Dad! Let's get you better, recharge your batteries, and get through this post-op. You'll see it won't be hard. You'll be back to work in a heartbeat, at home, with Lisa, uploading pictures that we've sent to one of your Picasa folders. Right? Do you hear me, Dad?

She registers, in addition to this, that a nurse asks

them to leave. They have to clean the wound and take his vital signs and carry out the other routine procedures. Her brother, her sister-in-law, and Vera go out into the hallway where Lisa is waiting with her two daughters. Vera realizes that Lisa is afraid too. They discuss the results of the operation, what the doctor said. Did he mention the forbidden word? They talk about what each one interpreted from that brief interchange. Vera listened, but she didn't repeat it: he'll live as long as he can live; he'll die from this. She heard it so quickly that she wasn't sure she heard it. Maybe the others didn't hear it. Maybe they interpreted it differently. She preferred not to repeat it, as if omitting it would eradicate that monstrosity that got into her father's body until they had to operate on him, force its removal. And why say such an ominous thing anyway, pronounce it aloud? That night, they'll all sleep somewhere else. There's no place in the ICU to stay. Luckily, tomorrow night, he'll be in a private room with a sofa bed. Vera will be the first to spend the night with her father. Then, they'll take turns, every day someone different. The second night, when Vera stays with her father, will be the second day since his operation. It will be Wednesday. It will be a different day.

# Day 2

Morning

Sleeping in her mother's bed is uncomfortable. The mattress has sunk in on one side, and the surface is uneven. All night, she feels like she's going to fall or sink into a dark hole never to return. The surface of the mattress is a light that overwhelms her even when the door is closed. The balcony of her mother's apartment faces east, flooding the house with sun very early in the morning. Her mother sleeps on the sofa bed. Or so she says, but she lies. Perhaps it's laziness, but Vera doesn't want to verify if she's telling the truth. Perhaps her mother says she sleeps on the sofa bed so Vera won't feel obliged to offer her mother the bed in her own house and lose that precarious and privileged space. Or perhaps to avoid another of the many confrontations that she has so frequently with her when they see each other in person. On the phone it's different. They don't fight. Vera rations out weekly conversations and saves up possible topics to avoid getting to the core of things. That's what she's always afraid of with her mother. Getting down to real issues, unraveling the deepest origin of her feelings. The origin of their disputes. A dynamic that began when she was a girl but has remained unsettled, forever incomplete.

*Notebook*

She opens its cover and places the notebook on the table, next to the mate, the toast, and the raspberry jam. Her mother prepared the mate and the toast. She set out the jar, sugar, and a knife to spread the jam. And a spoon. Oh, and also a paper napkin. Vera avoids her mother's eyes. But more than anything she's avoiding the sunlight that's slowly blinding her. I need a sun visor. Then she writes that when she woke up that morning the image of her father with his eyes open had become imbedded in her: his stiff body, his twisted hands, and his yellow skin. That image again filtered in, and now it haunted her throughout the passageways of her hours. And although she tried not to remember the trickles of saliva coming out of his mouth and the tubes and wires that tied his body to the metallic machines and the bags of liquids, she had to see him that way, completely stripped: the electrodes stuck to his hairy chest gathering the electric impulses from his body. White hair. As if the illness had no qualms about invading an older man, at the limits of old age. A huge piece of gauze covered his belly, but it did not cover the scar that cut across him from another surgery, a previous one. That was from the gallbladder. She couldn't imagine the pain he felt from the needle sticks and the scalpel cuts, taking out and mixing up everything inside. She imagined that this long and meticulous process would not go unnoticed. She closed her eyes because she didn't want to go on writing down her own fears. The fear that surfaced when she thought about such things. About surgical removal and what it means to take something away. The chromatic meaning of his pallor. The meaning of her presence in an unexpected place. Everything backward. Everything in a place where it shouldn't be. Herself in Buenos Aires when she should be in some city in the United States. Her brother in Pilar, when he should be traveling to Rome. She shouldn't be staying in her mother's apartment avoiding conversations or the displeasure of looking at her through eyes red from crying. She closed her notebook. She now began to take notes mentally, what she didn't dare to put down on paper, because writing is like spilling a glass of wine. Once it starts to spread, there's no way to contain it. It's a stain that expands until it penetrates some remote space and stagnates there, like words. Writing was salvation for her, but also a precipice. Something longed for but feared. She followed her mother with her eyes. Her mother had the TV at full volume. Always bad news and insecurity. And that person who was her mother—Vera's mother—lived in that world of violence, corruption, kidnappings, attacks, and assaults. A world detached from her own but that now returned in the form of dismay and discomfort. Vera was no longer a part of that world. She didn't share it. And her mother reproached her for it. She judged her because "if you're not here, you don't understand." She spelled out, on an imaginary page, that *Crónica TV* had an advantage that other programs lacked: no pretenses, it overflowed with grandiloquent and exaggerated lies, real deformities, and grotesque parodies of human misery. Everything unmediated. Pure and real absurdity, pure and absurd reality. She sketched out a wish for herself: ask her mother to turn off the TV, explain to her that all the commercials with loud sounds and incendiary words were bothering her, tell her she needed a change, to walk to the hospital. But she didn't say any of that either. She tore herself away from her notebook. She locked herself in the bathroom and breathed deeply in the dark. Silence, blackness.

On the Way to the Hospital

Straight on Bulnes to Santa Fe. Turn left and walk straight ahead: pass the Botanical Garden (full of shit and the smell of cat piss), Plaza Italia, Pacífico. Turn right on Fray Justo Santamaría de Oro. Turn left on Cerviño. Trinidad Hospital.

*Notebook*

Vera knows she carries a mental notebook where she keeps her impressions in words that later she will empty onto a blank page or into the yellow notebook in her iPhone. In Buenos Aires she carries a notebook to capture the changes that have taken place in the city where she was born. Another city erases the Buenos Aires of her childhood; she takes note of this as she walks. The Buenos Aires of her adulthood imposes itself on her like the image of her immobilized father in his hospital bed, his face looking at the ceiling. The Buenos Aires that she's walking through in a hot December has dead pigeons and smells like shit, human shit, excrement. Her hands take note of what her eyes capture: dogs peeing by her side, on a tree, on a wall, on tires of parked cars. Dogs on leashes and walking in groups of ten, fifteen, smelling each other, licking each other, kissing each other with their dog tongues, discharging fecal matter that inundates the steam that rises from the asphalt until it traps the city. Feces.

During Christmas week, the garbage collectors are on vacation. Vera observes how the waste accumulates on the street corners and in the dumpsters. She observes with distant eyes. Partly because the trash does not invade her directly. But, even more probably, because her father's image in the intensive care room clings to her like a preoccupation that completely absorbs her. That image is tied to her like a strap that doesn't allow her to move. It encircles her neck, her feet, and her hands. That's why, after carefully examining the mountains of waste, Vera understands that she needs another way to record and understand the changes that creep up both on the city where she was born and on her father. The world of her childhood that has changed irreversibly.

Discreetly she begins to capture the visual carnage that will give her a total of fifty-six digital images. She follows the trail of trash, excretions, and fluids that dogs, cats, and humans leave on the sidewalks of the port-city streets. She writes down ephemeral comments because some of them slip away from her and some she retains. Is it Vera who gets trapped in the chronological distance that transports her from her mother's house to her father's hospital? Is it really Vera who lets herself be carried along by these smells that inundate her visually, or is it Gisela who tries to grasp the ephemeral and transform it into verbal matter, memories and sensations that come forth as she walks and recreates a world that has disappeared? A world that begins to dissipate without her even knowing. The woman who proceeds, camera in hand coupled with her mental notebook, moves with agility because her movement occurs long before anything horrible happened. Long before. Vera does not know it, but she intuits that there is much more than discarded material in the waste that she photographs. She senses that what's being disposed of and what she captures is like a shadow of a larger and intangible materiality. But that omen doesn't yet have a foundation, and it only manifests itself as a high cloud in a red, incandescent sky.

While she walks, she writes that she will have to identify and catalog the material. And before she archives it, review it and group it into files according to formal and thematic categories. She, like a neophyte spectator, will have to sit down and look at a world that will open up and try to devour her.

At the Hospital

She arrives early. Earlier than her family. She signs in at the counter, goes up on the elevator to the third floor, and makes her way to the waiting room with sofas, next to the hallway and the door with the two little windows and a buzzer that gives access to intensive care.

Visiting hours are restricted. She doesn't know. A nurse tells her. There's no way to negotiate getting in. Vera goes down to the coffee shop and waits for her brother. They have to ask, complain, insist (beg?) for him to be moved to a private room where they can spend the night with him. Lisa arrives. They all go up, emboldened. Perhaps weak but with the illusion of demanding something fair. Something that belongs to them. They wait in the hallway because, before they enter, the doctor on duty will arrive and give them his report. All the doctors that come out of intensive care have the same casual air about them: the unbuttoned white coat with a stethoscope; a notepad where you can see a grid with names and different words, all lined up and crisscrossed, like a game of tic-tac-toe. A routine checklist where they keep an account of the status of the patients. If they've improved. If they've worsened.

Her father has improved. The report falls into the category of what is expected. There are no shocks. Nothing out of the ordinary. Improved means the opposite of getting worse, right, doctor? Or getting better?

When the young doctor on duty leaves, Vera, Lisa, and her brother remain silent. They wait for visiting hours, seated on the sofas in the waiting room, facing the elevator that brings up friends and relatives. Lisa starts crying. The nurse gestures that visiting hours have begun. Vera goes in first.

*Notebook*

It is Gisela who writes, slowly, the word "return." Or it's Vera. To return to Buenos Aires is to return to see my father lying in a bed, yellow. To see him and hold his hand. Gaze at him. Smile at him with a look that shows unexpected tenderness. Perhaps a cheerful tenderness. A tenderness as deep as the love that pushed her onto the airplane, to arrive running, out of breath, to kiss his forehead and promise to be by his side. To take care of him, despite him not wanting it. In his fatherly, infallible, and firm role that weakly reproaches her and tells her it was not necessary. Why did you come? How nice that you're here. You shouldn't have bothered. The kids? Your hands are cold. Are you okay? Yes, Dad, I'm fine. It's the air conditioning. Tomorrow I'll bring a sweater.

*Notebook*

Buenos Aires is different.

Another city erases the city of my childhood.

I need an image that erases that of my father, yellow.

I need to look for an image of him laughing.

Now I have one: I'm happy.

In the ICU

She felt the cold of the room. The window to her right looked out over the tops of the London plane trees. He didn't see her come in. His eyes were looking upward, half closed. She searched for the right tone to let her words spill out. A happy tone, encouraging. She couldn't betray herself, although, more than anything, she couldn't betray him. She couldn't let herself be overwhelmed by her feelings. Rationalize, she commanded herself, and hide your emotions. None of that weepy stuff or showing what you feel. It was an extreme command, and Vera obeyed, frightened. She entered quickly, smiling from ear to ear, and hugged her father. She didn't give him time to figure out who the person who had fallen on top of him was, kissed him, and whispered in his ear.

He was hoarse. It was hard for her to understand what he was saying to her. He was choking. He told her in a faltering voice. He felt something like phlegm in his throat, and he couldn't swallow. He kept insisting. Vera called the nurse to ask her to help him. Meanwhile, she squeezed her father's hand and told him what she had done that morning. She described the city according to her eyes, not the city he knew by heart. She rang the nurse button again. Are they treating you okay? What did you do this morning? The nurse still hadn't come. He complained again. The phlegm kept him from articulating his words. Finally, the nurse came. She asked Vera to step outside. Vera turned away, but she didn't leave the room. From a distance she tried to see how the nurse extracted the phlegm from his throat. What would she do? How? She saw her father's eyes roll back in pain; the discomfort blinded him. A woman in a white uniform pushed her outside. She closed the door in her face. She left her alone next to a counter full of monitors and cables. She walked away, turning her back on intensive care, and she imagined her father spitting out phlegm. The drains attached to the sides of his abdomen were already extracting a yellowish liquid. The phlegm must have come from somewhere else. She ran into Lisa in the hallway. Her brother had left and would return in a couple of hours. They both remained silent, seated on each end of a sofa in the waiting room. The sofa had beige and pink magnolias. Lisa always on the edge of tears. Vera giving herself silent commands. They went back in together when the nurse gave them a signal. The nurse must have been fifty years old. She had wrinkles around her eyes. Wrinkles from the sun and cigarettes. In Argentina people still sunbathed a lot. And they smoked. Not like in the U.S., where there were campaigns to protect yourself from the sun and where smoking was frowned upon. Her hair was dyed orange. She had two very long gold earrings. Vera thought they'd get tangled in her hair. Lisa asked the woman. She asked her about his condition, the status of Vera's father. His throat. Where was the phlegm coming from, she wanted to know. The nurse showed them a dental crown with an extensive root. It had come loose when they intubated him, and it fell into his throat. It got stuck. Probably the sides of the root got embedded in the internal membrane. The nurse put the crown in a container and gave it to Lisa. Keep it. Take it home.

*Notebook*

She didn't write it down, she didn't want to write, she didn't want to say it, not even think it. When she saw the crown with its tooth and its long, curved root, she almost stopped breathing. The projected smile that she had put on her face became an amorphous thing that could be weeping or an intense and strange feeling of uneasiness that kept her from articulating words. She refused even to register the sudden photo that imposed itself again when the nurse held up the bottle, and through the light she saw a crown that hid a tooth, but not its root. And the root was so long and pointed at the end that, when she mentally transferred it into her father's throat, a convulsion took over her body, and she had to leave the waiting room immediately. She excused herself to go to the bathroom and release what had been put inside of her and what her glassy eyes did not hide but her father must not see. He couldn't. He couldn't know. He had to see the light that was breaking on the horizon and not the difficult projection of a flawed glare. He had to trust her. And she was his eyes, his gestures, his expressions. She was the text through which he was decoding the illness that was engraving itself on his body. Might my father be able to perceive what my words deny? She wanted to know, among the mental scribblings and traces of gestures and clumsy attitudes. Might he know about my fake smile or my projected tone? Might he be able to read between the lines of what she herself did not know? Might he understand this deep and sharp sadness that suddenly emerges as an unearthly sorrow?

At the Coffee Shop

A friend came to see her. They had met at a conference in England, and now he was in Buenos Aires for a brief stay. The specific moment of this encounter is erased from Vera's memory. Perhaps because of the wait for the doctor's report or because her father had asked her, like a little child, not to be gone too long. Perhaps because the image of the tooth's root came back now like the image of the dummy that had been imposed on her or the image of a distant Buenos Aires in ruins. Her father demanded, or pleaded, for her to come back up quickly because the nurses didn't come right away when he called them. He complained. He would call them, and they would take a long time to come. Nothing matters to them, he would conclude weakly. A nurse dressed in a light-blue uniform standing next to the coffee shop door called out her last name. They're going to take your father to a different room, and they need you to collect his belongings. She said goodbye to her friend, promising she would get together with him before she left, and rushed up.

*Notebook*

Seated in a chair in the empty hospital room, Vera tries to pinpoint the true intention behind a notebook. I don't know why I write all this. Why do I talk about my father if I want to write about another person? To invent a character, someone removed from me. To write the story of a woman named Vera. Besides having a German name, Vera wants to reorganize the world so that it's as close as possible to perfection. In a certain way, she's obsessed, on the edge of manic. The best way to organize chaos is through writing. But Vera cannot write that story. Not even she, the monstrous creature she is. What she has become. Absorbed by domestic life, work, her kids. At night, Vera jots down fragments and outlines in her iPhone before she drops, exhausted, and falls asleep, or early in the morning, a phrase will filter through her mind and reflect the exact tone that comes to the surface, the right way to begin a paragraph, the words that will cause her to delve deeper into writing if she didn't have to stop, pushed into fulfilling her role as mother, researcher, and professor. At times it happens in the afternoon while she's packing the kids' lunches or the next day in the car when she's going to get groceries. If she doesn't write it in her phone she writes it on a napkin, on a paper filled with illegible words that become the to-do list. Write, write, write. A constellation of scattered fragments. How to begin to put the story together?

In a Private Room

He has a room that faces an interior patio. A hospital bed with monitors and a rod from which they hang the small cords and tubes that administer the medicines and IV fluids. A panel where a CaviCide-brand container of sharp objects also hangs. To the side of the bed, a small bathroom with opaque glass. Facing it, a silent television. Vera taped the drawings that her children and nieces and nephew drew for their grandfather below the screen attached to the wall.

She should go back to her mother's house to get her clothes. She should get her toothbrush, toothpaste, her contact lens case. She should remember her glasses. She should grade, at night, her students' papers and figure final grades.

*Notebook*

To grasp the precise instant when her father makes it to the room and she stands up, slowly, anxiously. How to translate that to her notebook if she doesn't even know what to say or when to move? A nurse asks Vera to leave the room. They're going to clean him up. Her father sees her, out of the corner of his eye, since his rigid body doesn't dare loosen the multitude of cords and wires that adhere to him, like an electrical panel that someone opens, leaving its contents uncovered. An amalgam of wires, cords, and conduits. He looks at her, and she makes a mental list: he's afraid. You're afraid, Dad. But I'm here, and I brought your razor, your slippers, your favorite pajamas. Now, once we get the doctor's report, I'll go to mom's and change clothes. I'll be back. She wants to note that part of reconstructing a world that's falling to pieces is to know, to verify, if her father will wear those pajamas again, shave again, walk slowly again in the slippers he bought in China, the blue and gold ones, with his hands behind his back and his prominent belly leaning slightly forward. She wants to write it down, but she erases it immediately because she knows that he will use all that she brought to the hospital again, and that question is inappropriate. Why get ahead of herself? Didn't Dr. Casabilla say patience?

The Afternoon Doctor's Report

Will he play tennis again, doctor? This time it wasn't Vera who asked. It was her brother, who had just come back and found her seated on the edge of the sofa they had moved from the private waiting room in the ICU. Her father's eyes were staring at the television, now on, showing an action movie. The volume was high; his eyes dissolved into the screen. Her brother made a sign for her to come out. She left her purse on the sofa where they would take turns sleeping at night until each one would take their place again in other lands and hemispheres, and she walked outside. But before she left, she walked over to her father and told him she'd be right back. He was half asleep. He wanted to sleep, but they woke him every half an hour, at least, to do their routine checks.

Lisa and her brother were talking with the doctor on call. A woman. She had the same attitude as the others. An unbuttoned white lab coat, stethoscope around her neck, a notebook with predetermined variables that indicated if the patient was getting better or worse. Normal progress, she announced. But is he suffering, Doctor? He's moaning. That's normal. That's why we're giving him sedatives. And Dr. Casabilla? When will he come to see him? That, I can't tell you. You should contact his team.

*Notebook*

Vera digs through the notes she took before getting to Buenos Aires, when she wrote an email to Dr. Casabilla, and he responded with the following:

Dear Vera,

Your father has a large-sized tumor in his pancreas. This has provoked obstruction of the bile ducts, causing choledochal syndrome (jaundice, choluria, and acholia).

I consider that it has been developing there for quite some time (months). A tumor marker, the CA 19-9, whose normal value should be less than 34, is at 4,600. It is very probable that the tumor is malignant.

The tomography reflects a large-sized tumor, but apparently it has not compromised other organs (metastasis), nor is it invading any important blood vessels (veins or arteries); that is to say, the data suggests that, along with the general good health of your father, there are no existing surgical contraindications.

The natural evolution of the illness—without surgery—generally carries a life expectancy of three to six months.

No further studies are necessary to determine the diagnosis or the treatment.

The most appropriate treatment under these circumstances is its resection (extirpation) and adjuvant chemotherapy, beginning forty-five days after the operation.

The feasibility of the resection will be confirmed during surgical exploration. The extirpation of the pancreas could be partial or total, depending on what is found.

The operation is complex, and, although the risk of mortality during the procedure is almost zero, it presents a percentage of approximately 20% morbidity and a minimal percentage—less than double digits—of postoperative mortality.

Having achieved the extirpation of the tumor and with everything going well, the patient will be hospitalized for no more than three weeks, after which the patient will reinitiate habitual activity.

I have tried to cover all matters related to your father's situation. You will be able to find more information on this subject or any word you may not understand on the Internet.

When I spoke yesterday with your father and his companion, I tried to be clear but to avoid the severity to which I am referring in this email. You will have to forgive my frankness, but I believe that, given the circumstances, these concrete data are necessary for you and your brother.

Sincerely,
Dr. Casabilla

Was this note a dream that arrived on her computer screen, and she accidentally erased it? Was it the fruit of her imagination? How is it possible that her father had been at her house, on a visit, and she had not noticed anything? Except that, at the airport, when she went with him to the departure gate, Vera broke down in tears, and she had no idea where they were coming from. Tears that suddenly took her completely by surprise, after her father turned around to look at her, to give her a last wave and disappear behind the security guards. Inexplicable sobbing that left her immobile, alone, and with a mysterious anxiety. A suspicion that, at that time, she did not know how to decipher. Perhaps it was the last time she might see him whole. In one piece. All of him in his most genuine condition as her father that came from afar to visit her, with his suitcase filled with gifts. But she didn't know it, nor did she predict it. She just let herself carry this strange anxiety around her like a halo for several days.

Round Trip

Vera leaves the hospital and walks toward her mother's house. The reverse itinerary. The light hits her eyes. And the heat. Spending all day with her father in the hospital stifles her, like Buenos Aires, which emits its habitual odors of excrement and pollution. Her mother is happy to see her. Seeing her in Buenos Aires goes beyond the reason for her unexpected visit. She's happy to have her at home. All to herself. But Vera doesn't share this happiness. She needs to talk, to vent. Without realizing it, she begins to cry. Her mother is chopping an onion. The television is blaring. One news story after the other: it's unsafe everywhere. Now her mother chops garlic. When she sees her crying, she turns and gives her a tray with some scones fresh out of the oven. Eat, it will do you good. My neighbor Cristina made them especially for you.

Night at the Hospital

She returned before it was time for dinner. She went up immediately, but the nurses were taking his vital signs, and they asked her to come back later. Twenty minutes will be fine, one of the women in charge of the floor told her. Her brother was downstairs in the coffee shop. He was also waiting. Vera ordered a beer. She needed to relax. She and her brother talked about logistics and planned new strategies for the future. Finally, her father was transferred to a room exclusively for him. That had been a feat. Above all because of how quickly it had happened. Her brother would spend tomorrow night with him. They hoped their father wouldn't become demanding like a child. They'd take it as it came.

When Vera went in, she noticed the noises in the room. The noise of monitors, plugs, a fan. Beep, beep, beep. It was summer, and it was at least eighty-five degrees Fahrenheit. The TV was also at full volume. It was hard to be heard. Vera moved closer to her father. His eyes were fixed on another action movie. He looked at her as soon as she came into his line of sight. Vera saw a spark of happiness. Then it went away because her father had his eyes halfway shut. He spoke into her ear. He told her he was thirsty. Very thirsty. There were cords and tubes hooked up all over his body.

*Notebook*

She should be grading. She should be reading the papers her students wrote in standard Spanish, not in the Spanish that now occupied her mind and that she used to communicate with everyone around her. She should be in front of her computer, correcting errors and typing exclamation points when a conclusion emerged, an idea, a comment worthy of note. Instead, she had a red pen in her hand over a yellow notebook. Writing about the thirst that was pursuing her father, she was trying to understand how that sensation of not being able to quench a thirst would be. She noted the nurse's emphatic denial when her father asked for water. She was a nice nurse, but firm and incorruptible. She looked like a nun, like the one in the movie *Ida,* which had the same beginning as *Viridiana.* It's normal for your father to be thirsty, the nurse explained to her when she noticed her accusing eyes from the other side of the bed. But the wounds in his body need to heal, she added. It's going to take some time, she concluded, and she immediately looked to another nurse who was bringing gauze and antiseptic creams to clean the incision that divided her father into two more or less equal parts. Vera noted: he is open,. everything is open inside. She imagined the stitches that were holding his flesh and organs, skin and fluids together. She thought about the water sliding down his throat. The plastic tubes that ran through an interior world of catheters and probes. She invoked darkness. There were probably noises. Possibly also colors. The nurse, trying to remain calm, looked at her again. She told her she would speak with the doctor. He'll explain how the sutures need to close. There can't be open wounds. For now, we will keep him hydrated intravenously. She didn't capture what the nurse said on the page, but rather in the look she directed at her father. She tried to make him read a more affable translation in her eyes, perhaps benevolent, different from what the nurse had just explained. But she didn't know how to discern how he had interpreted those coded texts that were from Vera's own eyes, the expressions of her body, the gestures and movements that spoke for her, on their own.

## Day 3

Dawn

IV fluids. The beep, beep, beep of the monitor is already an inherent part of the scene where her father's agony unfolds. Vera couldn't sleep; neither could he. Every thirty minutes, nurses were coming in to carry out their intensive care procedures. They came to empty his urinal. To bathe him. At six o'clock sharp a specialized team showed up to do an electrocardiogram. Vera counted the cords that were hooked up to his body. After talking with another nurse from the morning shift, she was able to convince them to give her father a bit of wet gauze that he could chew to moisten his mouth. She asked for ice, and, astonishingly, they granted her wish. Ice to quench his thirst. She imagined that thirst. Her father savored the wet gauze. He put it in his mouth quickly. They brought ice. He could put it in his mouth, they explained. But he should be careful. He couldn't swallow it. She noted that the yellow color began to fade. It drained from one of the tubes that was embedded in the left side of his stomach. She understood, when they came to bathe him, that the wound that cut across his body was deeper than she thought. The wound has to be cleansed, a tall, dark nurse dictated. It's important for it not to fester, he declared. Pancreatic cystitis. The pancreas is filled with cysts, said the doctor when he left the operating room. You can see it if you like. It is in the lab. Do you want it? Vera, her brother, and Lisa looked at each other, disoriented. Then they shook their heads. Nurses intervening in his body, talking among themselves, directing words toward her as she looked at them, bewildered. We have to increase the volume he's consuming, one woman indicated. Then she turned around and walked out. She wasted no time in returning. She brought small vials of nutritional liquid. She put the contents into the bag of one of the IVs that was hanging at the side of the bed. That should give him a little more, she described. They'll administer it along with his other medications. Beep, beep, beep. High-pitched sounds continued to escape from the monitor. The same woman controlled her father's glucose level. His insulin was going up and down. She called for another nurse, who came with a syringe. They took blood. Just a prick, that's all. Vera turned around and looked the other way. The TV screen glowed. It was on all night. An action movie. At full volume. Her father's arms filled with bruises. Purple disks, green and yellowish. Grading her students' papers was not easy.

*Notebook*

She writes in her yellow notebook that it bothers her to see her father's uncovered body. His body is not made for her to see undressed. The nurse asks me to leave and come back in five minutes. I give her ten. I don't want to see my father's body tangled up in cords and sheets. I don't want to see his smooth skin uncovered. His nearly hairless legs. His stomach dropping sharply toward a fuzzy orifice. She notes that her father calls for her, and when she comes in, they still have not bathed him, they haven't cleaned him up. He calls her to whine, like an obstinate child or a cantankerous old man. It's better to wait until they give her the green light before she enters. The nurses who bathe him prefer not to be watched while they work. She wonders, in words that she writes but chooses not to repeat, what these women think when they put their hands into her father's tender flesh? What do they feel as they extract cloths and gauze from the depths of his pale skin and collect filth from deep inside as they wash him and leave him clean again? Dedicated to their work, what runs through their minds as, quietly, they face something as somber and eclipsed as his bowel movements, his waste? What do they feel when their patients, all of them in different beds, let themselves be caressed by rough hands that run across their bodies? Do they feel love? Are they repulsed? Do they feel hate, devotion, solidarity? Or do they not feel anything? Absolutely nothing? A job they internalize and do day after day, mechanically, without a single thought, or without it occupying an instant of their precious time. I head to the waiting room. The sofa with beige and pink magnolias opens up and receives my exhausted body. I fall into it along with all my weight. I tumble down. I also let myself be embraced by an exhaustion that I still don't recognize but that I do begin to predict. There's an end table with a lamp on each side of the sofa. It looks like a hotel. Also, there are high pedestals where they have placed some simple and modern plants with little red flowers. When I return, the nurses are still there. I know because the door is half closed. I slowly approach. I look through the crack, and I see, once again, the body of my father lying there. They still haven't finished. He's still naked.

In the ICU

Lisa arrives. Her brother arrives. Vera needs someone to take her place. She needs to get out of the hospital, call her husband and talk to her kids. She needs to breathe. Her brother talks to her father about his businesses and economic situation. He explains to him that, when he's recovered from his surgery, he should retire, enjoy life, travel. His father agrees. Vera gestures to her brother. She notices that her father's getting tense because it's a sensitive subject. The economy and his work situation have been a source of stress for a very long time. Something bad that, little by little, has been getting the better of him. Her brother tells him a joke, and her father laughs. He calls for Vera; the three take a selfie, sticking out their tongues. Vera thinks this is childish, and, despite finding selfies extremely idiotic, she figures it's better not to say anything, to smile and make sure everyone is happy, to hold her tongue and avoid unnecessary scuffles. She tries to persuade herself that it's most important to smooth things over and not leave any space for friction. More than persuading herself, she commands it. Just another command she will have to obey. Even more so when she sees her father happy, seeing his children together, by his side, after so many years and so little time together. She can't prove it, but Vera notices those sparks that appear in his eyes when he looks at them, although he doesn't express any emotion and his rigid face remains motionless, looking at the ceiling or the TV where action movies play incessantly. Her reactions, her comments, her interchanges of ideas and strategies must depict a smooth surface. Avoid trouble. Don't fight. Enough, enough fighting.

*Notebook*

She writes that leaving the hospital and breathing outside air floods her with a sensation of relief. Navigating the cement tiles of the sidewalk, although they are plagued with shit, filth, and foul odors that concentrate in the air, has a positive effect. Juggling several things in the December afternoon fills her with a strange feeling, a state of mind that fluctuates between nostalgia, sadness, and happiness. This mood is not something she expected to find in this unrecognizable Buenos Aires, a city that has changed, although it still preserves all its familiarity. She insists, perhaps with a tinge of another color—purple or, even better, green—that navigating street tiles and smelling dog shit is like going back to another moment in her personal history. And she underscores, as if it hadn't been clear to her yet, reliving fragments from her childhood. Because shit has always been there, a witness to so many happy episodes. Shit from the past, she points out, is the same shit from the present and the future. But seeing passages from her past parade by does not frighten her. Caressing those fading remnants, like a whole life compressed into a few seconds, transports her to distant eras. To her childhood in a bilingual school. To her childhood traveling through distant lands. And a childhood of much solitude, but a happy solitude, surrounded by imaginary friends and real cousins, aunts, uncles, grandparents. People who would begin to vanish from her life and from the world. The tones of their voices, the smells of their bodies as they rub up against or embrace each other would begin to evaporate the moment she crossed the sea of exile, in the distance. She would begin to trim them with cuts from a pair of sharp and rusty scissors that leave an imprint on a face. She writes in capital letters, and without knowing why, that this afternoon she will see her friends MK and IS. They'll meet at the coffee shop on the corner by the hospital. She'll see them, after so much time without seeing them, and she'll hug them. And when she hugs them, they'll laugh, albeit briefly, about all the stupid things that humans do. Vera emphasizes in her notebook that she will be the person who will meet MK and IS. Or will it be Gisela? Will it be GH or GG? But then, what role will GL play? Who is she, Vera? And who is she, the one who's writing? Will they all be the same at one time? Which one of them, somewhat alienated, will crumble facing a table and a hot coffee until she dissolves into an ephemeral figure and evaporates into the blue and infinite sky?

Afternoon

Vera went back to the hospital, after showing her friends a patch of hair that turned, from one day to the next, completely white. The hospital whitened my hair with all its antiseptic treatments. The bleach of stress. When she returned, she found the nurses bathing her father, and she took the opportunity to go to the visitor's bathroom. After closing the door and making sure that it was latched, she looked in the small mirror and let her hair fall to both sides on her shoulders. Streaks and streaks of white were growing everywhere. She examined her scalp, surprised to find white streaks even beneath the most voluminous layers. She pulled her hair back again. She put it up in a bun to avoid the heat and perspiration on her neck. She breathed deeply. She had to put on a smile and show happiness through her eyes. She had to wipe off the anguish and any trace of sadness.

When she got back, Lisa was sitting on the sofa, arranging the things that her father had asked for. Her brother would arrive at any moment. He would stay with her father that night. It was Thursday. Friday was Lisa's turn. They were hoping he could be transferred to intermediate therapy soon. They would "upgrade" him one floor "up," one of the doctors on duty joked. The doctor's report would also come at any moment. Vera sat down next to Lisa. She noticed that it really did take a lot for Lisa to put on the mask, and Vera chided her. She loaned Lisa a mirror so she could see herself. Her father was sleeping very lightly, never deeply. Lisa had started to take care of her father's business. She was always in a hurry. "Business" was a euphemism: her father had been in bankruptcy for quite some time.

*Notebook*

In the visual archive that she's collecting during her long walks through the city, she underlines that besides the trash, one recurring element sticks out in her native Buenos Aires: thousands of dead pigeons. Pigeons leveled by speeding cars; pigeons fried by high-voltage wires; pigeons dead from starvation and thirst; pigeons poisoned by corn filled with pesticides; pigeons smashed by mischievous kids whose brains have gone crazy with all the existing high-tech digital devices; pigeons dead from the sadness of seeing a country filled with excrement; pigeons that believed and were disappointed; pigeons that bet and lost; pigeons that shat and were shat on; pigeons that grow old on monumental buildings and historic palaces: in the Plaza de Mayo, Puerto Madero, La Boca, Chacarita, Flores. Many, many pigeons, she concludes.

At the Coffee Shop

When Dad gets better, Vera said to her brother, we'll organize a trip to Miami with the whole family. Vera's father loves Miami. He goes to all the electronics shops, and they speak Spanish there; it's like being home. She suggested they should tell him, so he'd be encouraged to get better faster. But Dr. Casabilla finally came with his report and indicated that he continued to progress positively. And his glucose? Why does it shoot up so fast, doctor? It's normal and under control. And his temperature, doctor? It's being monitored. As soon as they finish bathing him, they will take a chest x-ray. Just to check. Routine. Dr. Casabilla tersely concluded the conversation and added: any questions, don't hesitate to contact my team. Team? When my brother tried to ask him again if he would be able to play tennis, there was no trace of Dr. Casabilla in the entire ICU waiting room. Vera, Lisa, and her brother went back to the room.

Her father was waiting anxiously. Even though he was weak, he could raise his voice and ask about his progress. Everyone put on the undaunted and serene mask and promised him that soon they'd be transferring him to intermediate therapy. His progress was ideal. He complained. He couldn't sleep. The pain, being uncomfortable in the same position. They woke him up every thirty minutes throughout the night to draw blood, to take his temperature and blood pressure. They'd make sure to ask for a stronger medication. Lisa showed him his razor. When they bathed him, they'd also shave him. "You look like an old man," she said and smiled. In a few minutes the nurse came in with her gloves and bathing cart. Lisa left the room and gestured to Vera and her brother to follow her. Outside, Lisa cried. She talked about a pulmonary embolism from sitting so long in the same position. It wasn't an unfounded suspicion. She connected it to the orders for a chest x-ray. She was hysterical. Vera's brother helped her to the sofa. Lisa ran her hand through her hair again and again as if she were trying to fix something. Vera brought her a glass of water. Lisa put a tranquilizer in her mouth. She swallowed it slowly. It was late. Vera started excusing herself to leave. She said she'd be back on Friday. Her brother would stay until she came back tomorrow morning. Lisa agreed. Her face was still pale. She dropped her shoulders and sank into the sofa. She sighed. She told Vera and her brother that she would tend to things at the store, and then she would head to the hospital. Not to worry. The three said anguished goodbyes.

*Notebook*

Trinidad Hospital. Turn right on Cerviño. Straight on Cerviño. Go around the U.S. Embassy. The checkpoints with dark windows and the local police posted on each side. Look to the left, toward the park and the mosque. The mosque that's right in front of the U.S. Embassy. Turn right on Colombia Avenue. Right again on Sarmiento. Plaza Italia. The Botanical Garden and its characteristic stench. Unmistakable stink of cat urine. A visual pause to register the shit on the sidewalks, the dog piss like threads that cross each other and overlap and the fetid blood of the rotting pigeons. She captured a total of fifty-two images. Waste, trash, filth. She focused on the canine shit. It was unsettling to see so much of it. Where does so much excrement come from? Not only did it smell of doglike shit, but also human shit. Straight on Santa Fe to Bulnes. Another stop, still on Bulnes, to examine the trash piling up on the corners, growing every day, reeking with the heat, mixing with the excrement of dead and living creatures, overflowing the dumpsters, piling up in front of the ecological Bulnes Eco Suites hotel. The corner of Güemes. Could it be that everything is absurd in this Buenos Aires that is so distant and at the same time dear and intimate? While she takes down these mental scribblings with her capricious observations, the doorman of a building approaches, cautiously. When she sees him, she discovers that he is angry about the spectacle of the trash or, even more probably, mad about finding Vera taking pictures. The man in charge of the building, perhaps with a feeling of fault, blathers about the trash collection unions that took an entire week off for the holidays and let the trash accumulate and get out of hand. But a neighbor, who was paying attention to the conversation, rants against the government, blames it for the trash that increases, measurelessly, in Buenos Aires, while a young Asian man, on the opposite corner, is detained by a group of aggravated police screaming at him, asking him, without mercy, to show them his papers. Hey there slim, you illegal? They yell at him. But the Asian tourist, who walked next to them a few minutes before crossing Güemes, doesn't understand and, frightened, covers his face with his backpack, afraid of being hit or shot. She notes, in her little yellow notebook, that Buenos Aires is a city that wants to be global. It's trying like a ten-month-old child who's trying to walk. However, it's an infant with coordination and mobility issues, and, although it tries, it will always be difficult. And she adds: there are foreigners everywhere.

# Day 4

## At Her Mother's House

The TV is blaring. The noise in the background from the morning newscast abruptly woke her. Where am I? she wanted to know. Could it be that I'm back home, with my husband and children hugging me tight in my bed? Could it be that I returned to the northern hemisphere, that I never traveled to Buenos Aires, my father never got sick, I never received that call pierced with suspicions and anxiety? Finding herself in her mother's bed, nonetheless, gave her a deep sense of unease. It seemed like a regressive situation. How strange, she said to herself. She should feel protected and loved. However, she felt out of place. She looked for her mother and found her in the kitchen, preparing mate. She had bought her Syrian pastries from the Once neighborhood. She had washed her dirty clothes. She had hung them out to dry on the balcony. After serving her the mate and the pastries and bringing her the kettle, she went to the bathroom to shower. Five minutes later she went to her room to get dressed, the room where Vera was sleeping and that her mother had given up for her. She told Vera goodbye and went for a walk. It was part of her morning routine. She would do some shopping. Do you need anything? No, thanks. The sound of the door closing, the sound of the elevator. Cristina, the neighbor, who says hi and gets in just at the right time. The whole house smelled good. Clean, but not with an antiseptic odor. Although three days had already passed since the operation, Vera had the same bitter sensation she'd had at the beginning. It was a taste that came back through the images she couldn't get rid of, but also through words. Words she put together in her own head until they formed sentences and ideas. Thoughts that swirl around, that swirl around her. When will he get out of the hospital? Will he play tennis again? An echo, echoes. And the final echo: don't hesitate to contact my team.

*Notebook*

Vera is the one who left Buenos Aires in a symbolic year, 2000, before the world came undone, to head to another country, another culture, another geography. Vera is the one who, with her enormous suitcase that a relative had loaned her, headed for the airport and said goodbye to her father, her mother, her brother. He would follow her in exile, although to other geographies, another continent. But it is also Vera who returned to this city that she left, and that left her to find her father lying in an ICU bed. And also, it is Vera who watches how the numbered buses from her childhood changed colors and shape; the 60, the 59, the 10, the 37. Even the routes had changed. It's Vera who now writes in her notebook that although Buenos Aires wanted to be globalized, it's a fragmented globalization, stumbling along, woven together like colorful patches and textures. A tapestry solid in some parts but more fragile and precarious in others. A tapestry full of holes. That is the Buenos Aires where Vera would arrive, with the porteños having a coffee at Starbucks while they walked down Santa Fe Avenue, with writers fascinated by the cumbia, with friends confronting each other about politics, not talking to each other, not looking at each other, losing any fondness, affection. Devolving into enemies. That's the Buenos Aires that Vera would land in. Or would it be Gisela? Probably both or all of them at once. And it might be the foreigners who were speaking Spanish with a different accent or a completely different tongue, the ones who were living with the bodies of torn-apart pigeons, shit and piss left by dogs on sidewalks, and spaces jam-packed with trash. Trash that would go on contaminating the air little by little until it completely absorbed it. In the visual diary that accompanied her notebook, Vera added the gash that cut across her father's stomach from one side to the other. She knew, nonetheless, that she would never have the courage to take a picture of it. She would memorize it and recreate it, she thought, but never be able to lift the sheet that covers his abdomen to keep that wound as an image frozen forever. Vera knew she was a coward. She never refuted it.

Midmorning

Vera arrived drenched in sweat. It was no less than eighty-five degrees Fahrenheit. Vera's brother was waiting for her in the hospital coffee shop, ground floor. Good news, he said: in a while they're going to transfer him to intermediate care. Then Vera knew that her father would get better. He would heal. When she went up to see him, they were bathing him. Once again, the door was half open and her father's body was half naked. Just a hint of his private parts between his legs, sheets being straightened in the agile hands of two skilled nurses. Her brother had already left. Now it was her turn. From outside she could hear her father's moans. He didn't sleep well that night, her brother had told her. He was uncomfortable, irritated. The heat made his unease even worse, and that demoralized him. Vera spied through the door. She saw the wound slicing through his abdomen, drains on both sides. She noticed that he had lost weight. His arms were bonier. His skin thinner. He was full of bruises. She wondered if this would be what many called agony. In the thick of torment. She turned around and sat in the waiting room, on the sofa with little beige and pink flowers. With her gaze lost in the opposite direction, she rested. She closed her eyes. She wanted to get out of that place and go far away. Not to see her father with purple arms and his body still, semimobile. The wound opened like an expanding striation and laterally cut across the entire surface of his stomach. The sheets tangled between his legs, his pale skin. His body, helpless. The sweat, despite the air conditioning. The heat that permeated from outside in until it installed itself like a thick and dark cloud in the nooks and crannies of the room.

*Notebook*

Returning to Buenos Aires. Returning to see my father lying in a bed, yellow. Seeing him and holding his hand. Looking at him. Smiling at him with a look that takes on unexpected tenderness, almost beaming. Tenderness as deep as the love that pushed me onto an airplane, running, flying, in a car, to kiss him on the forehead and promise to be by his side after surgery. An operation that would last at least six hours. Here I am, Dad. Can you hear me? I see you smiling at me. I'm smiling at you too.

In Intermediate Therapy

Vera and her brother agree to write to Dr. Casabilla. They must see him before they leave; if not, they won't have the opportunity:

> Dear Dr. Casabilla,
>
> I am writing because my brother and I would like to speak with you before leaving on the thirty-first of December. We don't have urgent questions, but we would like for you to give us a report before we leave, if possible. It would help us leave on a calmer note.
>
> Also, we wanted to ask if it would be possible to put some type of support bandage around our father's waist so he could raise himself up and at least sit on the corner of the bed to change his

position. The doctors mentioned this was a possibility, but they cannot do so without your authorization. What bothers our father the most at this time is his immobility; he is unable to move or change position. This, as well as a kinesiologist or physical therapist, would greatly help.

We will be here at the hospital all day today and tomorrow, but you can also contact us by email. I am copying my brother and Lisa on this email so that we are all aware of this communication.

I eagerly await your response and thank you in advance for your time and consideration.

Very sincerely,
Vera

They also discuss the possibility of providing her father with psychological assistance. Some type of therapy that will help him face the fact that he might not be able to play tennis again once he's out of the hospital.

*Notebook*

While she lets herself get carried away by the expected Buenos Aires itineraries, she puts together an inventory of things that grab her attention. On a list that resembles an enthusiastic scribbling, she writes that in fifteen years of exile she had forgotten the words "white chocolate en rama" or "white chocolate bark." She even forgot *that* chocolate, its flavor and its texture, although, more than anything, its existence had been erased from her memory. Walking in front of a store window and seeing chocolates "from Bariloche" took her back in time. Her adolescence, those years when she would sneak out of school, and her father, the very father who was now lying in a hospital bed, on his back and unable to change position, followed her and scolded her. One time he even threatened to check with the principal to see if she was lying, and he, her good-natured father, did so, getting her expelled. And while she's thinking about that, she goes back to that bark chocolate, the white chocolate en rama and the dark chocolate en rama, and she can't help but think about Ángel Rama. Rama the writer; Rama who wrote *The Lettered City* and *The Gauchipoliticos from the River Plate*. But for now, white chocolate en rama and dark chocolate en rama.

Intermediate Therapy

Vera gets a message from Lisa: *Are you at the hospital? The wound has started to fester in the middle, and they've covered it with gauze. His temperature went up, and they drew blood from both arms to get a culture. I thought your brother had told you. They didn't say how long it would take to get the results. I've been standing at the entrance to the bank for a while. It opens at 10:00 AM. There's a long line. Then I'm going to the clinic because I'm very anxious. xoxo.*

A few minutes later an email from Dr. Casabilla arrives:

Dear Family of Mr. G.:

Your father is progressing favorably.

If all goes well, this week we will be attempting to close off the nasogastric tube, begin to feed him, and remove the tube and drains.

At the same time, we will continue to feed him through the nasojejunal tube.

Earlier today, I spoke with the therapy coordinator to arrange for those visits.

It isn't necessary—nor convenient—to place a support bandage around your father's waist. I've already given instructions for him to sit up in bed and, occasionally, to stand (with someone present).

If you wish to have a personal talk with me, I suggest you come to my office at 12:30 PM so we can avoid discussing this at the hospital.

The address is 902 Callao Avenue, 6th Floor, Apt. E.

I'll wait for you there.

Sincerely,

JC

Vera turned off the phone. Her father was watching TV. Vera went up to him and took his hand. His fingernails had grown, like his hair that was long, white, and uncombed. She had never seen his hair so long. Perhaps it wasn't that it was long, but messed up, disheveled. Not without a certain mischievousness in his eyes, her father confessed that he was driving them crazy. Who, Dad? The nurses, he said. And he laughed, although just a little, because he couldn't move. His wound hurt. But weren't you griping that they weren't coming? I call them a lot. And he began to laugh again, like a happy child. And they come? she wanted to know. They complain and get irritated, he said. And smiled again.

*Notebook*

It's possible that Vera began playing the violin because her father adored the instrument. And she invented a genealogy that had her related to Jascha Heifetz, although her predilection was for the electronic violin, knowing she would never become a prodigy or a star in the music world. Vera wanted to enjoy the sound that emanated from the bow running across the strings, she wanted to carry her violin in a little black case and practice violin after having lunch with her father every Saturday and sharing a glass of wine with him. She writes, in her yellow notebook, that her father went with her to pick out the violin at a store in the Flores neighborhood where they sold used instruments. The person who sold it to them was of German origin, and he had a huge number of instruments hanging from the ceiling. All together, they made up a suspended universe of different figures and looks. A magical spectacle, like Gyula Kosice's Hydrospatial City. Vera recorded this information in her notebook while the memories entwined with each other, evoking days long ago.

Afternoon

Another message from Lisa: *I'm at the hospital now. Where are you? He asked for something to help him sleep, and they pushed what he takes at home through the IV. I talked to your brother about some psychological help . . . when your father couldn't hear . . . Tomorrow I'll call the OSDE insurance human resources' office. Your brother told me that they're taking his vital signs every two hours. They've already bathed and shaved him. For now, I'm going to go down and have a cup of coffee. We'll wait for you.*

In the afternoon, Vera got back from a walk. She needed to breathe some other air that wasn't as asphyxiating as the hospital's. After saying hi to one of the receptionists who now recognized her for coming in and out so often, she headed to the coffee shop, where her brother was waiting. Now that they were getting ready to leave, return, they needed to talk about logistics, separate emotion from empirical data, and develop a long-distance strategy. All three were going to see Dr. Casabilla at his office. After they spoke with him, they would decide.

*Notebook*

Vera wrote in her notebook with yellow pages that when she called her husband and her children on Thursday afternoon, she had talked about their abuelo, Buenos Aires, and their northern hemisphere vacation. Her daughter showed her, on the computer screen through which they were communicating, the little pink stuffed bear that Vera's father had given her when she was born. Her daughter showed it with such pride because it had been a present from her abuelo, and she had changed its name; before it was Mimo, and now it's Mima. But that, despite everything, he, or she, was still the same, with its little pink belly not so plush anymore from spending so many nights in bed with her little pudgy arms around it, the heat of her body and her covers. She also noted that her daughter started to cry because Mima's belly had been ripped open and urgently needed her mother to come home to sew it up. But since she wasn't there, she was far away with abuelo, Mima was suffering and now sleeping with her belly all open.

Night

It was Lisa's turn to sleep at the hospital that night. They decided that, afterward, her father would sleep alone because both Vera and her brother would be leaving soon, and Lisa would be exhausted from spending all that time at the hospital. When Vera and her brother went up to the intermediate therapy room to say goodbye, Lisa got upset again and began to cry. She waited for them in the hallway, in a waiting room that was different from the other one, while they bathed her father. He's impatient . . . He tells me, see, someone has to always be with me . . . because the nurses don't come when I call, and if I need the urinal, I can't do it alone . . . Lisa sat down. Vera and her brother sat down beside her. All three remained silent. They knew, Vera and her brother, that they would soon be leaving. Lisa would be alone, trapped in a universe of medical routines, injections, daily checkups. Seen from the opposite perspective, all three seemed to be disgruntled. Each one next to the other. Staring into the distance, their eyes lost in the ruts of a hazy thought. Lisa broke the silence. Finally, since the kinesiologist didn't come . . . the nurse sat him up and stayed with him for a half hour, but it wore him out. He gets tired even from talking, he runs out of air, out of energy.

*Notebook*

As she returns down the streets of her city, Vera thinks that Buenos Aires is laid out strangely. Or perhaps it's her visual diary that can't retain what her eyes are wanting to assimilate. While the world that gravitates around her is accentuated, her childhood slowly falls further and further behind. Like the transverse wound that bisects her father's abdomen, there is a Buenos Aires that is fractured between reality and memory. Vera examines a pamphlet repeatedly posted along a gray wall on one of the poster panels on Avenue Juan B. Justo. It reads: "Patria Grande." She notes the anachronism of the signs, empty signifiers that run along the streets as if it were a ghost city, tying invisible universes with equally invisible threads. Already nonexistent universes. Next to the succession of signs appears the word "resistencia." She questions, perhaps mentally: Resistance to what? To living and letting live? To laughing? To having fun? Resistance as a stance? Empty, affected, hypocritical resistance. Who's in charge of the right to resistance and the right to resist resistance? To disobey the premise of resisting because it is a well-known, conventional resistance? And perhaps, doesn't dictating resistance imply an order, a ruling that requires submission, compliance? She notes, in italics: I resist resisting. I do not resist. I do not obey. I do not adhere. Long live anarchy.

# Day 5

Early in the Morning

Vera got there early in the morning. The nurse on duty was acting as if they were in a military regime. She wasn't speaking. She was howling. Lisa had already submitted to the dictatorship of the early morning and was obeying orders. When Vera arrived, Lisa sighed a breath of relief and hugged her tightly. She then said goodbye. She'd go home to take a bath and get changed. She'd come back at noon. Vera would have lunch with her brother at the corner restaurant next to the hospital. The military-style nurse was ready to bathe her father. She ordered her to leave the room. Vera didn't know how to respond to these decrees. She thought about her father, about his body, subordinate to the nurse's regulations, lying in a metal bed covered with white sheets. She had already seen him half naked. As he was convalescing, his nudity transformed into something different. It was strange to see him that way. One of the doctors from the surgeon's team came in and examined him. Worried, Vera explained to him that her father had been nauseated that morning and he had thrown up. The doctor asked her to wait. He indicated that he would take out a drainage tube. That would leave only one. Since she only had a few days left in Buenos Aires, Vera promised her father she would stay with him at the hospital on Monday and Tuesday. If there was anything he needed, just let her know. That morning Vera had cried. She had hidden from her father so he couldn't see her. She pretended like she was going to get the nurse. When she returned, her eyes were red. When her father asked her what was wrong, she invented something: her contact lenses were irritating her. She faked that she had to leave again to go to the bathroom only to return after five minutes to show that she had cleaned, rinsed, and put in her contacts again. Her father couldn't see her cry. He mustn't. It was not permitted. Her father must see her happy, and Vera's eyes, she kept telling herself, marked his progress. His evolution. His improvement. If he saw her cry, she would never forgive herself.

*Notebook*

It is my brother who, now, looks deep into my eyes. He looks at me with both of his turquoise eyes. But he also looks at me through the eyes of his children. They observe me while they entertain themselves with their iPads or they devour an ice cream from the Persicco ice cream parlor. Is it possible that I can no longer translate what I feel into something different from what I'm trying to say? My gestures also betray me. They are subtle, but they say more than what I had wanted. She notes that having lunch with her brother and her mother on a Sunday when they hadn't planned it is strange, a strangeness that is difficult to classify because it doesn't refer to anything, she writes, to anything that happened before. Neither had she prepared herself mentally for this. To the contrary, the occasion imposed itself unexpectedly, almost violently, without giving Vera time to digest it. We walked through Palermo like when we were children and lived next to Las Heras Plaza, or the "penitentiary," as we used to call it. We walked down the transformed streets, stores that remain in my memory but were demolished, turned into businesses that resemble those you see in other hemispheres; it's the globalized part of the city. She writes: Who will remember that where Persicco is now, on the corner of Salguero and Cabello, there used to be an old store that sold brooms and cleaning products, even lawn chairs and gardening tools? An old bazaar, with two worn marble steps at the entrance and huge store windows on each side. We walked down those passageways that had become new spaces, and we tried to pull back the veil that hid what was beneath their brick, cement, and granite facades. Perhaps what we were looking for was the past. To tear back the cover that would help us hold on to time inscribed on walls and streets that no longer exist, whose physiognomy has been disfigured. A past in which one also found my father, and it was he who, taking my brother and me by the hands, took us on a Sunday to the playground and the swing.

# Day 6

At the Hospital

Vera did not go back to the hospital after lunch with her brother, sister-in-law, nieces and nephew, and her mother. That afternoon she felt a fatigue that forced her to go to her mother's house and rest. To try to sleep. To relax. To occupy her mind with something different. She almost went to see a movie, but she decided to read in bed and let herself be taken over by drowsiness. The next day she went to the hospital earlier than usual, overwhelmed by a feeling of guilt because she had abandoned her father the afternoon before. She had sent a message to Lisa. She had explained how she was feeling. But Lisa, too, was exhausted. When she got there, she noticed that the same soldierly nurse from the day before was taking care of her father. She had square glasses that got Vera's attention. Her father was better. She asked him if he was okay. He was still in intermediate therapy, but he was now able to sit up in bed, with the help of a kinesiologist. If only there were kinesiologists in the hospitals in the United States, Vera said to herself. There everything was physical therapy or chiropractors. Her father sat up to see her. With her help, he could sit up for longer than the day before. He didn't feel dizzy or nauseated. But he grew tired very quickly, and he needed to lie down again. Vera wondered if, despite the militaristic nature of certain nurses, they had a special vocation to care for sick people. This nurse, although she seemed like a sergeant, let a certain compassion slip through the symmetry of her glasses. She hid it, but one could see it by the care she took as she lifted her father, twisted his body, and laid him back down. The most complicated part of her job was moving the tubes out of the way, the cords that kept up with the beats of his body—translating them to the monitor—the intravenous fluid. Once he was lying down again and comfortable, her father was able to rest. He would watch TV, or he'd close his eyes, trying to sleep. Until, in thirty minutes, they would return, to get a culture; take his blood pressure; make sure his intravenous nutrition hadn't run out; or check if he was hydrated, alive, breathing, or needing to be cleaned up.

*Notebook*

Throughout the yellow pages of her notebook, she kept notes on methods employed by doctors to keep the bodies of patients clinically alive. Alive, despite losing their faculties; alive, though their brain no longer functions; alive, though most of their organs stop working; alive, though consumed by fatal bacteria. Alive: while the heart beats, they will be kept alive.

Intermediate Care

Vera and Lisa exchanged the following messages:

L: The doctor on duty just came by. He doesn't like how the wound looks . . . he said that it seemed a little swollen. He said that he was going to talk to the surgeons to see if would be advisable to take a CT scan and see what's happening inside. *They can't let us be happy for one minute . . .*

V: I'm almost there. Keep me posted.

L: The doctor from Dr. Casabilla's team came by just now and closed off the tube that goes to the stomach. He said he would try . . . If he's not uncomfortable or nauseous tomorrow, they'll take it out. Now he can't have any water. Only ice chips on his lips. He told me the doctor on duty had gotten in touch with him, and he didn't think it was necessary to take the CT scan. The infection is not caused by the surgery but by one of the catheters. They'll keep watching it. Now he's sleeping. xoxo.

V: Okay. I hope you can take this chance to get some rest.

L: His bowels are still moving, and it seems a little more often. When the nurses change him, I'll ask if it's diarrhea. They changed to a larger dressing where the wound is a little infected, and they changed his antibiotic to a stronger one. xoxo.

V: Let me know what they say. How many times did he go today? I know that he went once this morning . . .

L: And twice in the afternoon . . .

V: Yes, it's best to ask.

*Notebook*

Where are professional ethics? And bioethics? Where are the principles that govern biomedical ethics? Keep the body clinically alive, no matter the price, the additional cost, the collateral consequences. Is this by chance the foundation upon which modern medicine rests?

Dr. Casabilla's Office

Lisa and Vera took the bus that would leave them two blocks away from Dr. Casabilla's office. After walking under the burning December sun, they entered an old building, with a gated elevator and high walls and ceilings. Her brother couldn't get there on time from the north part of the city. Lisa and Vera introduced themselves. A woman behind a tiny little window wrote their names down and invited them to go into the waiting room. Antique furniture was all around the room, and the wooden moldings on the ceilings and in the fireplace were original. There were fashion and healthy-living magazines. Other people were sitting and waiting. Vera wondered if they all had cancer, like her father. She wanted to know what their situations were and why they were all seated there, waiting. However, instead of asking and talking, she preferred to remain seated in one of the pink velvet reupholstered chairs, in silence. She didn't even talk to Lisa. They already had their questions ready. Her brother sent quite a few others when he found out he couldn't be there. Dr. Casabilla hadn't given them many options, and they didn't want to leave without having a personal meeting. After waiting an hour, they were called by the secretary, who directed them to the doctor's office. He greeted them warmly, leaving any arrogance for other occasions. To all the questions that Vera and Lisa asked, he always answered that progress was positive. However, he suggested, we must wait and be patient. Patient! Vera exclaimed to herself. And the infection, Doctor? Your father is fine, progressing with a probable infection—under control—in his wound. Because of this, we started antibiotics yesterday. Today it is less distended. All of this is expected in the context of a major operation, to which he was submitted. Rest assured. I will inform you, by email, of the basic developments as they occur. Have a good trip and happy 2015.

*Notebook*

She writes that it seemed strange to walk down Callao Avenue. The names of the streets—Marcelo T. de Alvear, Paraguay, Córdoba, Viamonte, Tucumán, Lavalle—sounded a little strange. They reminded her of other days, other years, other visits. But more than anything she seemed more disconnected from them. As if the person walking down those streets and reading the signs were a foreigner. A foreigner who recognizes the streets but who cannot associate what she sees, observes, and perceives with what she remembers. As if the relationship between memory and reality had been interrupted. A short circuit that perturbed her, but (and this she highlighted in another color) she didn't know if it was coming from inside or outside. An alien, in the sense of a foreigner or extraterrestrial. That is what she writes: extraterrestrial.

# Day 7

The Last Day

Vera woke up in her mother's apartment. In her mother's bed. In Palermo. In a Buenos Aires filled with smells and steam that extended in all directions. She didn't eat breakfast. She would eat at the hospital when the nurses asked her to leave the room so they could bathe her father. In one of those breaks she would take the elevator and go down for a coffee. From her mother's house Vera took the habitual route she had taken all the other days, this time without stopping, not even visually, to take in what was around her. The idea of departing and leaving her father in the hospital occupied her mind completely. When she arrived, she went immediately to the intermediate care floor. She looked for a makeup mirror she had in her purse to see if her mask was on right. In the hallway that led to her father's room, a patient was walking with the help of a family member, while nurses were coming and going with the daily rush. She adjusted her smile, breathed deeply, and knocked on the door. Since no one answered, she went right in. Her father was dozing. The TV was turned up to full volume. Vera went over and lowered the volume with the remote control. He had spent the night alone, as he had done since the three of them kept their promise to spend one night each. He was still uncomfortable and had trouble changing positions. Lisa had written that his wounds were getting infected. Vera couldn't see them or know how they looked. To do this, she would have to pull back the sheet and, with his abdomen uncovered, examine the dressing. She didn't dare. Besides, her father was sleeping, and that prized moment of rest and happiness could not be altered. She saw, nonetheless, his uncovered forearms that rested on both sides of his body. They were full of bruises from all the continuous tests to evaluate his blood, his red blood cells and his white blood cells. She kissed him on the forehead and said: Here I am, Dad; when you wake up, you're going to see me, and I'm going to smile a big smile that you're going to remember even when I'm gone. And even when I come back to visit you, you're going to remember it, because my smile is going to say that I'm here, Dad, don't go. Wait for me. I'm almost there. Please.

(Here)

December 31

Vera said goodbye to her father. She said goodbye to her brother, his wife, and their kids. She said goodbye to her mother. Before she got into the car, they made up with each other. Vera and her mother fought every day, only to make up afterward, as if time hadn't passed. As if Vera kept being an adolescent and her mother a mother of an adolescent. After an embrace in which they exchanged glances that were laden with love, guilt, and regret, Vera got into the car that would take her to the Ezeiza airport, which, for many, was also the "Ministro Pistarini" International Airport. The driver talked nonstop. He told her about his daughter, his son, and his girlfriend, twenty years younger. Vera didn't want to talk. But she nodded while he spoke so as not to offend him. Since private car drivers in Buenos Aires were armed, she thought it was better to get along with him. It was New Year's Eve, and Vera imagined a deserted airport. The holidays were something serious, and the entire country would celebrate until they couldn't celebrate any longer, until they were worn out, until they threw up on the sidewalks or ended up in the hospital with burns in their eyes. Families would shut the windows of their apartments so the fireworks and individual firecrackers wouldn't fly into their houses. December, she thought. A word loaded with familiarity: with memories, with the past; with smells, with tastes and images; with feelings associated with heat, people drinking beer in pizzerias, outside, cheerful, happy, spending their paychecks, partying. Nevertheless, Vera was mistaken. You got it wrong this time, babe, she said to herself. The airport was full, packed. People everywhere. And to top it all off, she was returning through Miami. Everybody in Argentina went to Miami in December—where else? All the people from Argentina were lined up out of control, disorganized, impatient, and hyped up. Empty bags to fill with purchases in the mecca of Latin American capitalism. Plain suitcases awaiting their lunches and dinners on Collins Avenue. On Lincoln Road, in Bal Harbour. But not Vera. She was only passing through Miami. She was a passenger in transit who had to change flights so she could get to the arms of her husband and her children.

After waiting in line and boarding, Vera sat down and looked out the tiny little window. The light from the sunset had faded, and in its transparent rays, she saw her father's face. Already night, she only saw the shadows of the dense, hot clouds and more and more tiny lights from the huge city. Buenos Aires was a twinkling map that got smaller and smaller as the airplane soared into flight and surrendered to the air currents, the stars, and a moon that was shining more than usual. A woman from the United States sat beside her. She didn't speak Spanish. She explained to her that her son had fallen out of a tree, and she had to make an emergency trip because he had been hospitalized in the Fernández Hospital. She was an older lady, plump, and nice. Vera nodded, but her mind was soaring, like the airplane. She closed her eyes. She needed to rest.

*Notebook*

In her yellow-paged notebook, she writes that the image of her father, like a paralyzed dummy, right after the six-hour operation, woke her up. And if she screamed, she notes, the noise of the engines rescued her from the possible looks of reproach from other passengers. The woman in the seat next to her was snoring, and most of the passengers were sleeping or watching movies, lethargic. Bodies with blank minds. Vera deliberates. Buenos Aires is changed, she writes, and this new city was slowly erasing the city of her childhood. She realizes that as she writes, she reminisces. Writing is reflecting. She underlines the last part. She speculates about writing, about the written word, and now, back in the airplane and back to herself, the Vera or the Gisela who once dreamed about being a writer, realizes that urgency to write, to become a writer. She notes:

> A writer who does not write is a being who
> kills him or herself little by little.
> Perhaps that writer is me.
> I am a disarray of matter.
> Nothingness that no one wants to pick up.

She looks at her notations, she flips back and forth between pages. She reads: "Do I write or not?" Then, on a separate page, another quote from Clarice: "I wanted to write a book. But where are the words? All the meanings have been exhausted." Her father's image, she notes, returns like that of a ghost. An immobile ghost, with hands folded, rigid. Will she be who she was before boarding the plane that took her to Buenos Aires? Will she write a coherent manuscript, a well-constructed, conventional story, or will she be limited to inconclusive narrations, incoherent fragments that resemble metaphysical digressions and reflections?

January 1. New Year

Vera finally found an image that would erase the one of her yellow father, remove his bruises, the intravenous tubes, his body's nakedness intertwined in the white sheets. She looked for a different image, and she found the one that Lisa had sent her: her father smiling, his eyes overcome by the brilliant blue of happiness that she could not feel but that she recognized and that relieved her. Shifting it and inserting it in another space helped her mitigate the images that were so vivid from when she was in Argentina. She arrived one day before her husband and children got back from vacation. They had gone without her, or despite her situation. That day, she could concentrate on getting the house back in order, her things, her world. It was winter, but it was a mild cold. She lived in the suburbs, and her house was like any other house in any other suburb. All the same: monotonous, with a front lawn, with sidewalks (or not, depending on the neighborhood), with a backyard. In some houses, sumptuous yards unfolded, but hers was simple, with few bushes and unarranged flowers. She fixed something to eat and then went to take a nap. She had jet lag.

She woke up and didn't know where she was. The house was cold, and Vera was shaking beneath the blanket. She felt hot and cold at the same time. When she got up from the bed she tripped over a toy and fell to the floor. Night had not yet fallen, but the light of day had dimmed, and now a sort of zenith prevailed that represented day's end, or, better yet, night's imminent arrival. Disoriented, she walked to the kitchen and made herself a cup of tea. It was strange to be in the house alone, without the kids shouting and talking or asking her a thousand questions at the same time. And there she was, drinking a cup of tea, with exacerbated slowness, and wondering, as she looked at her face reflected in the windowpane, if the future is already written. And if it is written, she continued, will it be indecipherable? We will never know beforehand what will happen. How to know it? How to guess it? How to know if her father would play tennis again or not. If he would travel to visit her again; if he would come, at least one more time, to see how her kids are growing, to watch them play soccer in a Messi jersey that he had bought them as a present, to see them go swimming, put on a play, go to a party, or celebrate Thanksgiving; to watch them play piano, go bowling, or, simply, go to a movie. Simple things. But those were the bricks, the daily fabric that life was made of. What you create every day that then goes by—maybe too quickly—that become memories: fragmented images. Some more tangible, others more ephemeral. Some tossed in the memory bin, others framed on invisible walls, decorating the temple of Memory, uppercase M. Seeing them superimpose themselves, overlapping, on the film of memories, generated in her the same—exact—impression she had when the whole family, together, watched the Super 8 movies her father took himself or acquired. That's the way they watched many of the Disney classics, like *Peter Pan* or *Alice in Wonderland.* One after the other on a huge white screen, set up in the kitchen or living-dining room, depending on the occasion, at the apartment on Las Heras and Canning (today Scalabrini Ortiz) where she had lived all her life until she left to live alone. Charcas and Bustamante. Then to the northern hemisphere. It's strange, Vera noted, that having grown up so close to the cinematic montages, homemade or amateur, that her father would put together, meticulously, every Sunday, she had not been interested in professionally pursuing that destiny that maybe still was assigned to her. Because if the future is written, she thought, perhaps it will say in some part that she, Vera, will follow in her father's footsteps and record, without ever stopping, countless hours of film: landscapes, people moving slowly against urban or rural backdrops, magnified and distant objects, all with a typical slowness of the nouvelle vague. That's the way her father liked it, so much so that his audience often dozed off. They would yawn or get up and go to the fridge to look for something to eat or drink, distracted, automatic. Could it be that her father did it on purpose? Might he have enjoyed those prolonged scenes in which all was silent, the sound of physical movements and the rustling of natural elements? She thought her father could have been a good film director, if he had a good screenwriter who accompanied him. Or, perhaps, a cameraperson. She remembered that she and her brother would snicker. And many times they would laugh. Now she remembers everything as if it happened yesterday. As if time were a brief caress that, like a wave, approaches quickly and then subsides.

*Notebook*

She writes that her father is still in the hospital. He's still laid out in the room where she left him. She tries to guess what might be going through his mind. How might he see the world from that hospital bed, with intravenous tubes invading his skin, catheters and electrodes connected to his body? Seeing the world from a bed in a hospital in a city in a country in a continent in a world that who knows how long it might be there? How long will it be there for him? She underlines that writing does her good and she would like to write a piece about her father, about how it feels to succumb to the carnage of the medical system to which he was subjected and about a world that makes or does not make sense. She doesn't know. She doesn't know? Yes, she knows.

But she doesn't want to write it. Instead, she wants to write that her father smiled when he saw them, when she and her brother got there before they took him into surgery. That he was waiting for them. That he griped at them for coming and wasting money on flights, but that complaint was an excuse. It was pretended. Deep down, he was happy. She saw it down deep in his gaze. In his two sky-blue eyes like the waters of the sea, not turquoise, like her brother's, but sky blue, like those of a calm sea. She also saw his fear. A fear that his voice tried to hide but that every now and then would betray him. How could he not be afraid? How not to be frightened before being put to sleep with narcotics and letting yourself go, docile, under the knife, to let your body be cut and sectioned off by expert hands, gloved, precise? Cold. She traced in her notebook a desire in the form of a heart with childlike handwriting in the center: I love you, I'm thinking about you.

Day No Number

When her family got home, Vera met them with tight hugs and kisses. Vacation was over and they had to get ready to go back to school and the routine. Vera thought the routine would give some sense of order to her daily existence, and, maybe, the possibility of blocking off some time to write. Her book about her father would be the story of his life: a man who married a woman who wanted more than what marriage could give her, a passionate man who slowly began to be worn down due to the daily togetherness of marriage combined with the constant ups and downs of his country. He had a family and success as a businessman, but then, starting after the divorce, which coincided with several social, political, and economic events, he was dragged down to an uncertain place, a world from which he had become detached some time ago and to which he believed he would never return. Like many Argentines, his economic standing changed, like his social standing. A man whose passions were turning into resentment. A man who couldn't separate the external from the internal, nor avoid that, in the end, what was outside would infiltrate his life, his body, and finally, his blood: the cells that would lead to the drama of his fate. It was strange to think about it like that.

That night, Vera couldn't sleep. She woke up often, eyes wide open with a clammy forehead. She grabbed the phone and wrote: "A house full of boxes; a dead father and two children running all around. An absent spouse, far away, in a foreign country." Then she let herself again be embraced by that slow and warm drowsiness that did not submerge her completely in a distant universe, but left her exhausted, half asleep, between phases, soporific states. She thought she was delirious, but it was an internal delirium. Vera didn't know what she was writing. She was not interested in identifying the meaning of her words, either. Having a phone at her side with a tiny keyboard was one of the wonders of technology. The rest was trash.

After a half hour she woke up again. This time the phone vibrated on her nightstand, and the screen lit up. She had received a WhatsApp from Lisa:

*I'm glad you made it home. The night at the hospital was rough. Your father went on himself several times . . . he was embarrassed to keep calling the nurse. It wasn't diarrhea, so everything's okay. The nurse told me that since they had given him Reliveran (to stop the vomiting), it also helps his bowels move. Another kinesiologist came by and sat him up again like yesterday. He could only take it for an hour, and then they laid him down again. He fell asleep. They drew blood again and gave him more antibiotics. They still haven't come by to give me a report. They haven't told me how his white blood cells are either. And Prego, from Casabilla's team, hasn't come by either . . . I wanted to talk to him about the tube they were going to try to take out. They bathed him, and I asked them to shave him so he would look better. I explained to him that I can't spend the night . . . that I'll come by before going to the store and after . . . but I need you, he says. Being really dependent doesn't do any good either, right? I'll be taking care of things as they come. I hope. If anything new comes up later, I'll write you. xoxo.*

What time was it in Buenos Aires? What time was it where Vera lived? Was she up in the middle of the night or was Lisa? Or both? She turned the phone off. She put it in the drawer. She closed her eyes. Her husband was sleeping. Her kids too.

*Notebook*

She noted that when her daughter got back from vacation she started sobbing in her arms. Mima, her teddy bear, had its tummy cut open and Vera hadn't been there. She hadn't been with her to heal her Mima. She sat down next to her and began to sew the stomach of her little bear, the pink plush toy, with pink thread. The little bear her father had given her daughter six years ago. Her daughter treasured, dressed, and fed it. Mimo before, now Mima (Vera was unaware of the origins of its names, including the reason for its transformation) had a hole in the middle of her tummy that went across from one side to the other. While Vera sewed stitches on Mima's tummy, her daughter observed her out of the corner of her eye, looking out for the fate of her little bear. She didn't seem to have much confidence in the stitches. Something, deep down inside, was not very convincing to her. In her notebook with the yellow cover, Vera writes that, despite the distance, her father's and the little bear's body are waiting in a horizontal position, simultaneously, to heal, to restore themselves, and to become what he or she always was. She writes: "The daughter-mother looks at the little bear and rests her eyes on the metal needle, small, sharp, imagining other sharp instruments and other perforations. The little pink teddy bear has been her daughter's favorite for six years. She must save her. If her cut grows longer, her daughter will not forgive her. The origin of Mima's sadness will reflect on her." She closes the notebook. She scribbles between tangled thoughts and incoherent ideas that her father is still lying on his back, even though Lisa writes to her to tell her that he sits up thirty minutes a day.

Day No Number

Another WhatsApp from Lisa:

> *They keep giving him a broad-spectrum antibiotic. They've already found one bug that's infected him, and there are two others that are spreading but still not identified. He's still got the nose tube, but they've promised to take it out . . . Casabilla didn't come. The kinesiologist came and sat him up like before. While he was up, he was able to swish around some sparkling water to loosen up his saliva that had been stuck for ten days. You can't imagine what he spit up . . . he felt like he was drowning, and, to add insult to injury, there are two tubes that go down his throat, so he can't clear it . . . to cough up any phlegm . . . He was worn out. He's still got more down there, but when they sit him up tomorrow, he'll do it again. It was like he had worked at the loading docks all day. In half an hour he was so tired that they had to lay him down. He also told me they came to give him an electro when I wasn't there. Tomorrow I'll come around 11:00* AM *and stay till night. He made a slight face when I told him I was going home to sleep . . . he's afraid . . . I told him that no one was going to make him walk on his own . . . not to worry. xoxo.*

Within ten minutes, Vera's brother sent her a private WhatsApp to coordinate things and talk. Besides the group text with Vera, her brother, and Lisa, the two of them kept up a private conversation in which Lisa didn't participate. Without saying it, Vera knew what it was about: offering psychological support for their father. And for Lisa.

*Notebook*

She writes, going back to her notes from before: What will my father think when he finds himself lying in that bed, his family far away? What images will run through his mind? What memories? Will he remember when she was barely two years old and would play in the sand with a pail and shovel in Mar del Plata? Will he remember that he and her mother had taken that forty-five-day trip to Europe? She and her brother were left with her mother's parents. Every week she destroyed the gifts that "arrived from Germany... France... Italy...," throwing them from the balcony that looked out over Las Heras Avenue, paying no attention to the complaints from the neighbors, the doorman, and the people who were waiting for the bus below, from the parents who were picking up their daughters from the Catholic girls' school on the corner. Vera, refusing to pee as a protest against her parents' abandonment and indifference, having to be taken urgently to her uncle's office (her then pediatrician) to make sure she was all right, that she wasn't going to die of a urinary tract infection. Her uncle, the pediatrician, died in 2004 of lung cancer. Father of two children, both newly married. How much history can fit into the life of a human being? And will my father think about my children, my nieces and nephew, my brother, me? Will he think about what they put into his body and what they've taken out? About how his body will adapt to the absence of organs? About how his body will function without them? Without a pancreas, without an intestine, without part of his spleen? Or will Dr. Casabilla keep everything confidential until he recovers? And meanwhile, will my father dream about tennis matches, about trips to the United States, and seeing us all in Miami, tutta la famiglia unita, about a cookout with friends, where money problems don't matter? Or, to the contrary, will he concentrate on how the tubes they've stuck in his body bother him and how, surely, they irritate his throat, his trachea? About the brutality of the nurse who, in a moment of carelessness, ripped out the tooth implant he had in the back of his mouth? My father, what will he think about?

Day No Number

Another WhatsApp from Lisa:

> *I'm completely coming apart at the seams . . . Your dad is very demanding . . . He doesn't want them to sit him up if I'm not there, at least two times a day. The different doctors don't have a schedule, and your dad can't remember what they say . . . Today they gave him another electro, his glucose shot way up, they gave*

*him insulin and a blood thinner too. You can imagine the situation all afternoon and into the night . . . the infectious disease specialist came in to explain about the bugs—germs they found in his blood; she looked at the wound, checked the tube that he had in his neck, and made the comment that the tip of that tube also had the same germ that is common in the intestines . . . At the same time, I was on the phone with Casabilla, who called and claimed he couldn't come in because he had car trouble, but that he had spoken with the head of therapy that morning, some Suárez guy, and that he had ordered them to begin to give him sips of water to see if he could tolerate it. I told him I didn't know anything about it, and he said that he's human (Suárez), and that he could have forgotten to tell me. He says I have to begin to give him some water! I go to the nurses, and they tell me that if it's not in his chart, they can't give him anything . . . when the doctor on duty comes in, they'll tell him about it. Maybe this Suárez guy forgot to write it down . . . but in the meantime, he jumped down my throat. The infectious disease specialist was going to see if she thought an echocardiogram was necessary since those little bugs can also take up residence in the heart. She seemed to think your dad's abdomen was a little inflamed. He's taking some very strong antibiotics, and his white blood cells are slowly going down. At the same time, I've got to answer emails, write WhatsApps. Your dad tells me that when I finish writing the book, he's going to ask me something . . . If you guys don't mind, I'll write an email a day to both of you with the doctor's report unless there's something urgent that happens before . . . and if all of this weren't enough . . . I have to be at the store . . . And this is all just starting, even though we've already been in the hospital for exactly fourteen days. xoxo.*

It wasn't Vera but her brother who answered immediately and insisted on some therapy or psychological assistance. She, to the contrary, couldn't react so fast. She was paralyzed and wanted to return to Buenos Aires. She wanted to go back and be there, at her father's side, despite all the obligations that were keeping her from it, starting with her children and her work. Her husband probably thought she was going crazy. She spent all her time sending messages to her brother, contacting friends who were doctors, and surfing the web trying to find an answer or a clue that would lead her to a cure for her father. At night, she put her phone on the nightstand and slept with one eye open and one eye closed in case Lisa or her brother, whose continent was seven hours ahead, texted her with news. In the mornings she'd forget to fix the lunches for her kids, to answer the emails from her students. She got departmental meeting times confused, and one day, she almost went to class in her pajamas.

*Notebook*

She notes that she's the one who needs therapy. Buenos Aires appears to her at night, with the image of her father: his emaciated face, the intravenous tubes, the bruises, his yellowed, then pale, skin. The sheets entangled in his legs, his nakedness. His look, severe, sweet, or terrified. And then, she notes, Buenos Aires reappears with its habitual odor of shit; the shit of the dogs that shit on the sidewalks, and no one picks up after them; the shit of uncollected trash that sits stagnant facing the astonished looks of the people who live near the Eco Suites hotel on the corner of Bulnes and Güemes. Fragrant Buenos Aires. Decadent. Full of flies, cockroaches, and rats. Shitty stink of dog piss. Shitty stink of cat piss. Shitty stink of people piss. Human shit. Shat on. Buenos Aires is shat on. Everywhere.

Day No Number

In her office, Vera wrote down the title of a possible novel: *Imperfect Present.* Then she scratched it out. She was waiting for a student who wanted to discuss his grade on the final paper. Vera graded the paper at the hospital, the night it was her turn to stay with her father. That night, she hadn't been able to sleep. The nurses came in and out. The night nurses were two tall and muscular men. They had to be, because they were moving her father from one side to the other. They picked him up and put him down as if he were a light pillow. They bathed him, they helped him change position, they uncovered him, and they covered him up again. Everything every thirty minutes exactly. And her father, for his part, had the television blasting. One action movie after another. Arnold Schwarzenegger, Bruce Willis, Matt Damon, Don Johnson, Sylvester Stallone. Old movies and new movies. And her student's paper had not seemed good enough to get her attention, to get her out of that uninterrupted routine, even temporarily. To the contrary, distracted and apathetic, she looked up after finishing each paragraph, and automatically glanced over at her father, the nurses, or the TV screen: a woman in danger, about to be freed from enemy hands; a man who, even though he was being tortured, kept his integrity, unaffected and unchanged when facing insults and pain; a narco being ambushed. When her student came in, Vera, defeated, gave him his paper with a higher grade.

WhatsApp from Lisa:

> *Yesterday, the doctor on duty came by, but she only told me that his white count had come down a little and that there are still some bugs that are growing and can't be identified. When I learn more, I'll let you know. His bowels keep moving like crazy! I'll let him know you say hi. xoxo.*

And another, thirty minutes later, approximately:

*An intensive care doctor came by and told us that he thought the antibiotics were having an effect. I'll go home to sleep and come back in the morning. Huge hugs to all of you!*

*Notebook*

She writes that her father recorded everything on film. Super 8. Then videos. And after that, digital films. All that her father recorded is now in a pile confined to a closet in his house. He always wanted to digitize them. She notes: All those faces, what are they made of? Will anyone ever look at them again? What will become of them if no one ever shows those films again? She remembers the projector, the screen that unrolled vertically against the wall, far away. The lights that were turned off and the sound. More than anything, she recalls the projection: a raspy, continuous sound. She remembers the texture. That spotty texture, black and white, then in color. But never HD, always a visual hoarseness, like our lives: a continual hoarseness, raspy, continual, spotty. A pigmented film. She notes, on the verge of exhaustion, that the roughness that makes up each continuous tape that is her father's life, or everyone's life, is at the same time a noisy and deaf concatenation, both visual and blind, a gestation that radiates light, but often ends abruptly with that sound of the loose Super 8 projector. And then comes silence, darkness. The spottiness disappears. And the pigmentation takes on the fabric of a dream.

Day No Number

Vera entered the classroom where she was teaching a Spanish creative writing class. Her students had worked on a short story that they would read aloud. It was really a workshop. Vera had just gotten comfortable in her chair when she felt her phone vibrate, and she saw the light flashing: a WhatsApp from Lisa. Upset, she excused herself. She had never done this before, and she felt her behavior was deteriorating.

> *He didn't have a good night, and he's sleeping during the day. He gets upset when I speak to him because he can't answer. They sat him up, and I gave him some water . . . He could tolerate a half of a small glass. At least he didn't throw it back up. The kinesiologist came and made him do some breathing exercises . . . She told me he should do them several times a day. They keep torturing him drawing blood for cultures. It was already the second stick . . . the first showed those typical intestinal germs that I told you about. The wound is still a little infected. They still don't make him walk. The doctors on duty change daily, and there are no reports like they gave us in the ICU. I got here at 10:00 this morning, and I'll leave around 9:00 tonight . . . like yesterday. He says his butt is completely flattened, but he can't turn on his side. As to the support that you all are suggesting, you'll have to ask him, and if he doesn't even have the strength to speak*

*. . . he doesn't want visitors . . . I don't think it will be appropriate right now . . . Anyway, I'll keep it in mind . . . We'll deal with that later . . . He has the TV turned on to music . . . He doesn't have the patience to keep up with any series or the action movies he's always liked. Yesterday marked two weeks that that we've been here! As to the store, there's no doubt that his health is the top priority, although I have to get the tax payments ready, and when it's a lot of money, I don't send the employees . . . I make them myself, and if anyone leaves to go pay them . . . one person can't stay alone at the office . . . It's not that simple. Tomorrow we'll start a whole new week . . . I'll see how I get by. Hugs to all.*

WhatsApp from Vera:

*Would it be possible to hire someone to stay with him for a while during the day and to help him with the exercises while he's sitting up?*

WhatsApp from Vera's brother:

*Maybe the therapy can also be given to family members to help support the patient in getting through this time, and it could give you a little more strength than you have. Don't forget to check into it.*

WhatsApp from Lisa:

*I won't forget to check into it. When they sit him up, I'm here, and for the exercises too. If I repeat anything to him, he looks at me and makes a gesture like . . . don't bust my balls. They sit him up just two times a day. If there's nothing written in his chart, the nurses don't take any responsibility. It's all one long day for him . . . no breaks for, like, breakfast, lunch, a snack, and dinner. He just raised up the bed so he could drink a little water. He already put it back down, and he continues to sleep . . . xoxo.*

And immediately:

*I just ran into the nursing supervisor for the adult ICU, and I asked her about support, and she told me that it's a little too soon. We have to wait. She visits daily, and I'd already run into her a couple of times. She also works at the Hospital Italiano, and she promised to give me a card, which she just gave me. She told me to talk to Pardo, who's the head of that type of therapy. xoxo.*

Vera noticed that, as the days went on, she began to feel sorry for Lisa, because Lisa was her father's wife, but she wasn't her or her brother's mother. Lisa was diligently taking care of him, with his idiosyncrasies, and his children, who, at the same time, were far away and were pestering her with emails, WhatsApps, and phone calls. Lisa, assuming an unthinkable amount of responsibilities night and day, now had to take care of everything: rewrite all of the doctor's reports so that her father's family, out of the country, could be kept up on his condition, his progress and relapses (this included her father's sister, who lived in Germany, but not his brother, whose children, Vera's cousins, had forced him to move to Paraná when they found out he was suffering from Alzheimer's); deal with all the banks, employees, and buyers; pay the taxes and the debts; answer calls from family and friends who insisted on visiting her father even when he said emphatically, categorically, no. Lisa, who suddenly became LISA, a Super Woman-woman, was not accustomed to being delegated these types of responsibilities. Lisa or LISA's childhood was over, and she had to become an adult. Vera noted that her father didn't delegate anything to anyone. His world was his business, and every component that made it up moved under his exclusive directive. And even if her father'd had to delegate a mass of obligations to the woman he currently lived with, naturally (because there was no other option), it's probable for her to think that his two children should return to Buenos Aires and take care of him. They'd taken off. Or perhaps she thought the opposite: it's better that they're far away, so she could take charge of Vera's father's fate and manage the situation any way she wanted, doing nothing more than consulting with the family as a formality. How was Vera to know? But then, why was Lisa talking to them, making excuses for herself, as if she were being tested or looking for approval? And if it wasn't that, why was she writing them, overwhelmed by all the responsibilities? Maybe Vera and her brother should go back, take charge, lighten the load for Lisa; be by her side and next to their father. Maybe both of them, their father and Lisa, needed their support. Vera then realized that it was imperative for her to talk with her brother. Lay out this problem. Talk it through with him.

*Notebook*

In her notebook she scribbled random thoughts about Lisa. If she's strong, if she's weak, if she'll be able to go it alone, or if she'll need others. While she writes, she remembers that in Buenos Aires, she, Vera, had to console her. Vera or Gisela. She thinks she's weak. But in situations like these, one gathers strength. Strength comes from the most unexpected places. Perhaps even an unknown strength that is nothing more than a self-preservation instinct. Does Lisa have that instinct? And she writes, besides, if Lisa weren't Lisa, and the woman who accompanied her father were her mother, she would probably make her pay some way. She'd make her feel guilty. More her than her brother because of that unconscious rivalry between women. And for the tacit assumption that daughters must take care of their parents, the sick, children, others. But, she notes, how will Lisa make them pay in return? What will she latch onto in her desire for revenge? Her father's life, his dreams, his memories, his objects?

Day No Number

Vera sent a WhatsApp to her brother:

*I'm thinking about going to Buenos Aires. Lisa is overwhelmed, and we need to give her a hand.*

WhatsApp from her brother:

*You're crazy. Dad's going to get out of the hospital soon, and he's going to get better little by little. We can offer to pay a woman to help him. That way, Lisa will be less weighed down with everything she has to do. You've got your job, your family. Same here. Let's see how this goes, and maybe we can all plan something together. That will be better for Dad than going right now. Also, he just saw us. And that made him very happy.*

Her brother's message relieved her briefly. She was home, getting things ready for her class the next day. While she was making herself a cup of tea, she found a nature magazine that her children were reading. There were pictures and information about different animals. What most got her attention was a picture of a crocodile. It was calm, hiding under the water, its eyes protruding, its skin fused with the environment around it. A twilight landscape, almost nocturnal. She thought: Whoever took that picture must have been an expert at spying on crocodiles. She read that they have rather inactive lives and that they remain immobile for most of the day. In the morning, crocodiles search for the heat of the sun on riverbanks. They open their mouths wide, which helps them warm up. They don't have tubes or catheters, she thought. Because their blood vessels are close to the surface of their skin, heat passes quickly through it or from the outside environment into their blood. At night, water gets cold slowly, so crocodiles spend those hours in the river to keep warm. How lucky those crocodiles are, she said to herself. Despite having heavy bodies. She imagined a big crocodile, fat and inactive, lying at the edge of a river at night, conserving the heat it had accumulated all day long through its open mouth. She imagined its hidden eyes, almost spying, looking at the world from that immobility, that heaviness. When the kettle began to whistle, she poured the hot water into her glass cup, where it found a tea bag, and she returned to stick her head into the books she needed for the next class. Not like a crocodile, but an ostrich. There she was, trying to forget about the beauty of crocodiles: a beauty that, certainly, is rarely seen, until one electronic ding after another sounded on her computer. She had the stupid idea of posting a "congratulations" on the Facebook page of a friend whose book had just come out. The sound distracted her. She got up to silence the computer, but she ended up clicking on the comments that kept coming and making the perturbing dinging sound every time someone answered or added another congratulations.

And worse: that conversation led her to another page, and another, and then to others. Until she got lost in that black hole of images and words.

*Notebook*

She notes: I read, and I get bored, and I stop reading on the second, third line. So much crap is published today! She writes that she doesn't want to turn on her computer; she doesn't want to check her email. She writes: If I open the computer, it's to write, to draft an outline of my novel, but not to look at Facebook. I don't want to listen to other people's ideas. I'm not interested! I don't want to know if XLH had a baby or is on vacation in the Caribbean. Nor if JFW had a bad night from eating too much. I don't want to know the ideology of my colleague at the university or that of my childhood friend. I don't want to know that my uncle's cousin is a lesbian and hates straight people or that my neighbor thinks that all immigrants are idiots and should be beaten and killed. I don't want to be a witness to the public reaffirmation of their beliefs. Of that false and gratuitous pretense. Of self-congratulatory posts with pictures that other eyes will envy and comment on with posts filled with false emotions and exclamation points. No! Why did they invent Facebook?! To see the face of stupidity in its most naked version? To see and be seen. To be seen and become eyes that spy, windows into intimate, private worlds. To see what others have and what they don't have, to see their walls, their paintings, their tables, their books, their cats, their dogs, their babies, their schools, the horizons they photograph, the clouds they go through, the planes they get into and out of, their houses, their friends, their families, their cars, what they're reading and how they think, what they think, if they think. To see and become eyes. All Facebook is eyes that look, and they look at you. Eyes, eyes, and more eyes.

She writes: The novel I'm going to write will be called *The Passion According to GH,* and it will be signed by Vera Wang.

Day No Number

If the title *Imperfect Present* occurred to Vera, it's because ever since she was a girl, she wanted to fix what's broken, unfinished, defective; visualize a perfect world in which everything operates with precision. Her world must be synchronized, assembled, and constructed with precision and efficiency. It is not coincidental that her husband once asked her if she were Prussian. But Vera remembered her critics, lovers of chaos. She thought about those internal anarchists that frequently yelled at her about chaos being more creative and dismissing her utopian dreams as total garbage. Vera sensed that she suffered from obsessive-compulsive disorder; that explained a lot of things: the anxiety created by the lack of harmony in the order of the books in her library and the furniture in her house; the uneasiness generated by the food that was not lined up symmetrically in the refrigerator, in pure balance; or the hangers that must have the hook facing in one direction and not the other, the wooden ones together, then the plastic ones, and finally the metal ones; and her clothes, arranged by colors and categories, like her shoes. Any error, disproportion or anything lacking equilibrium as a whole perturbed her profoundly. It didn't let her sleep.

*Notebook*

She writes that chaos wins, it overthrows her, it overwhelms her. Her office accumulates papers little by little, like a body that keeps growing bigger, expanding. When her students pass by her office door they walk faster, afraid of being devoured by the objects that keep increasing: mountains, piles and piles of papers, books, letters, brochures . . . She notes, mentally, that one day a colleague will come by, or even the dean, or the president, in person, and they will look at her askance. They will examine her suspiciously and think she's losing her mind. That her office is unpresentable, like her face ransacked by the bags under her eyes and her disheveled hair . . . And on top of the brochures, banana peels, cookie wrappers and cereal bars, tea bags, spilled and dried yerba mate, green stains on papers, on copies of articles, on the university magazine, under apple seeds, documentary catalogs . . . Hoarding, hoarding, hoarding. Hoarding doesn't translate very easily to Spanish: "compulsive storing" maybe. If at times she suffers from obsessive-compulsive disorder, at other times she suffers from "compulsive storing," aka hoarding in English. She writes that she's compulsive: that's the common referent. Gisela is too. Another shared trait to emphasize. Or is it the Vera of her notebook? She points out that her compulsion can fluctuate, go in different directions. Even in opposing directions, mutually excluding each other. At times chaos wins, she writes again and underlines it with a red marker that spills out a mucus that she cannot identify. Then, she concludes, anxiety occurs without warning.

Day No Number

Vera composes an email for her father's doctor, Dr. Casabilla. She thinks she needs an official report, since Lisa is emotionally overwhelmed (or perhaps Lisa is only an excuse; she needs them to assure her that her father will soon get out of the hospital, that little by little he'll begin to walk, to play tennis, to talk to them on the phone, to Skype on the computer and even—who knows—travel to Miami to fulfill his dream of seeing the whole family together on Lincoln Road):

> Dear Dr. Casabilla,
>
> I hope these lines find you well.
>
> I write because I wanted to ask if, when you deem it convenient, you could send me a report with the latest news with respect to my father's progress. I cc'd my brother and Lisa so that we are all up to date.
>
> From what we understand, my father has begun to eat solid foods, they have removed the

nasal feeding tube, and he has also begun to stand up. To us, all these small steps are signals of how he is improving day by day, and we are, even from far away, constantly supporting him so that he will continue to progress in that direction. However, because we are not in Buenos Aires and are unable to have ongoing discussions with the doctors, we do not know how he is progressing from a clinical perspective. In particular, we wanted to ask you if the infection he has is internal or external and if you have localized the reason for and place of infection through tissue cultures. If there is anything else that we do not know and that we should know, please do not hesitate to bring it to our attention.

And by all means, I want to thank you very much for your time.

For now, I leave you with the kindest of regards.

Vera

Immediately, a WhatsApp from Lisa:

*They still haven't taken out the feeding tube. It's still there but without the liquid nutrition. I wrote to you all earlier that they have to evaluate if what he's eating is enough or if he's eating normally during the day, and then at night they give him food through the tube that's still there . . . that's what they told me when I was there this morning. xoxo.*

Good news (finally!). Vera gets excited, but then she deflates like a balloon that someone pierced. She doesn't know. Is it really good news, or not?

To whom it may concern,

Your father is stable and progressing favorably, considering his underlying condition.

Due to the fact that he is tolerating oral nutrition, today, I have removed the feeding tube that was bothering him and that has now served its purpose.

I spoke with the intermediate therapy coordinator so they can move him to a general care floor when there is an available bed.

We will see how he progresses in the next few days to determine how we should proceed.

Sincerely,
JC

*Notebook*

She notes: I feel abandoned in a sea of uncertainties. She adds, then, that the "underlying condition" to which Dr. Casabilla refers is pancreatic cancer that got into his body without warning. She had always thought about death or, maybe instead, about the end, the ends, but to see death that way, translated into illness, into degradation and agony, into paralysis, that she had not expected. To contemplate death is to think about it abstractly. To talk about it in the same way one writes about it: like when it happens to someone else. A banner headline on the front pages or an image that is conjured by the imagination. A projection, too, that acquires depth and density but remains in that sphere, that of fantasy. She writes: Dr. Casabilla, why didn't you get directly to the point and tell us, from the start, that the "base illness" that our father suffers from is a wild and voracious animal driven to pitilessly devour its prey? It rips out flesh, the desire to live, the desire to pick up the phone, the cell phone (which is more comfortable for someone who's flat on his back) and talk to his family, to his children, to his grandchildren, his childhood friends, and to cheer up. Happiness itself. It even devours that. And you, eminent doctor—no more of a doctor than I, let me tell you. I also, even though you may not consider it so, I too am a doctor—why did you not speak more frankly, why did you opt for this lack of transparency? By revealing the truth partially, opaquely, and ambiguously. I say this because you're playing the fool, pretending like you don't know something. Tell me, doctor, why did you not inform us that our father suffers from an illness that can cause a blockage in the pancreatic and bile ducts and produce jaundice, a condition in which the skin turns yellow? Why not, my dear little doctor? And then, after making a complete clinical "stage classification evaluation" and you and your team determining if the cancer can be removed through surgery (assuming, in this case, that it has not spread to other organs like the liver, the stomach, or the spleen and that it has not affected the important blood vessels, and that the surgery will be carried out through an abdominal incision that will remove the illness, the cancer, through a surgical procedure commonly known as pancreaticoduodenectomy—or the Whipple procedure), why did you not tell us that the cancer was still there, that the carnage was in vain, that the four weeks of degradation and lying on his back were not necessary? She notes that her novel is going to be called *The Devoured One*. Or, even better, *The Devouring Imperfect Present*. She was always bad at titles; that's nothing new. She writes that to title is to summarize and condense. She's also bad at that. She notes that it doesn't matter. One title or another doesn't change anything. The only thing that matters is her father and that fucking novel that she wants to write and that gets her all worked up. Why write? Writing is starting a conversation with the universe. Entering another dimension, one that, perhaps, can rescue you—all of humanity?—from an underlying condition that is pancreatic cancer, but, at the same time, from all cancers: superficiality, materialism, greed, slander. She wonders, through her notebook where she scribbles ideas, aphorisms, and isolated thoughts, if perchance she is not becoming a guru. Those of the Pacífico neighborhood in Buenos Aires who sacrifice chickens in four-by-four apartments. She, from the other hemisphere, imagines, dreams, fantasizes. Her husband may be right when he's afraid she'll go mad.

Day No Number

Lisa wrote her to say they'd already changed his room and moved him up to another floor. In the jargon of that hospital, to move up a floor meant a promotion, and a promotion, in that same jargon, means to get better. Progress (but Vera didn't believe in progress). She said they took out the tube, and he seemed like another person: *Really, he's brand-new*. He forbade Lisa to tell them, since he, alone, wanted to surprise them. So, please keep it secret. She understood how anxious they were and wanted to prepare them to hear the news from him. Changing the subject, she explained to them that since he no longer had the feeding tube, they had left a form for her to write down the amount of food that their father was ingesting daily. That way it was possible to evaluate the calories he was consuming. More good news, at least for Lisa or her father: they had let him have a diet juice drink. It was important for her father to drink lots of liquid. And for him to exercise, sit up for long periods, move his legs, try to stand up, and stay standing. And to try to walk. The kinesiologists were going to help him, she said, because he was getting so tense. He was aware of this, but his fear was overpowering. She wished them a good night. She was happy; she sounded happy. And with that, Vera became happy. She sent a message to her husband: that weekend they should go to the movies together. Or to the theater. She cleaned her office, threw papers into the trash, picked up the books that had piled up on the floor, and returned the ones she didn't need any longer to the library. She watered the plants, washed her teacup, ran a cloth across her dusty desk, updated her office hours, since the department coordinator never did it and her students always showed up after she had already left. She asked the janitor to run the vacuum cleaner since the yerba mate and the dirt from the flowerpots were forming a small garden on the corner of her desk. And she threw out the catalogs that came in large quantities, making Vera mad because she thought about all the wasted paper, the trees that had been cut down and, again, the progress she didn't believe in that invariably led to destruction. She cleaned her mirror and looked at herself in it over and over again: she examined her gray hair, the bags under her eyes, her disheveled hair. She had to get herself together since the departmental meeting was going to start in five minutes. What would her colleagues say about her unkempt appearance?

*Notebook*

In her notebook, she insists on asking the same question, as if the question mark was lying in wait for her. What would her mother have done if she would have had to take care of her father? Would she have made them pay over the long term or the short term? Would she have made them come back? "Made them" is a euphemism. A simple expression. Would she have played the victim until she made them feel guilty, responsible for being gone, for not being with her at such a moment, for staying with their families? Would she have stalked them psychologically with words, subtle glances, sarcastic insinuations? The unanswered question grows larger, like its punctuation mark, and now reappears under new forms, perspectives, horizons. Because what would the relationship between her parents have been like if they hadn't divorced more than twenty years ago? Would it have been like those marriages that work by inertia, or would it have been a loving relationship, a love they learned, rectified? Would they have negotiated their differences? She closes the notebook. She throws it on the floor. She looks at it. Mentally, she wonders how a counterfactual story helps her. She picks it up, annoyed, and opens it again. She notes, on the yellow pages, that her mother and her father were divorced, and Lisa, who wasn't her or her brother's mother, assumed a more distant position. Lesser? Lisa couldn't reprimand them like a mother would. That disciplinary role belongs to a unique character, and Vera cheered up and noted it with colors and glitter: How lucky she was to have only one mother and not two. The mere image of a maternal duplication made her gag. But she didn't want her happiness to dissipate. So she highlighted in her notebook that the way Lisa was making them pay was reasonable. You'll just have to wait, she noted, and see how it ends.

Day No Number

Viviana called Vera from California. Just like that, unexpectedly, without warning. She didn't even consider that she was violating the protocols of telephone etiquette that implicitly govern daily social interactions in the northern hemisphere. In the northern hemisphere, when someone phones someone else, they usually let you know. You arrange the call by email, or you send a text message. Vera suspected that this formality might be caused by the different time zones of the fifty states and Puerto Rico. However, Viviana's anger over a Facebook post overshadowed any such considerations. She told her ("told" is the narrator's courtesy, because really, she screamed) that a colleague of hers, at her own university, had commented that Middle Eastern terrorists were heroes of a revolution that they didn't understand. An invisible revolution, or one that was not visible to them. And they, Viviana screamed at her on the phone, were Western (uppercase W). And since Viviana was a hardcore feminist, as they say in the northern hemisphere, and she had dedicated her life to feminine emancipation not only in the West (uppercase W) but around the Globe (again, uppercase), she was planning to write a letter to the president of her university and lay her cards on the table. Vera told her that the posts she was seeing on Facebook seemed more infantile to her than irreverent. And many times, obsequious. Brownnosing. For example, she explained: If a person were well known or had a job at a prestigious university, the posts came with excessive exclamation points. As if those who used them had not matured.

And as if those who answered them were not analytical. As if everything they had read had ended in infantilism, and, in the end, a certain emotional politics took over formal relations and transformed them into interactions that were more applicable to high school: with adoration and condescension, which also provides a lot of drama. But Viviana was still extremely upset. It seemed irresponsible to her. It's not only that they are childish or idiotic—that was inoffensive enough—but to brazenly celebrate what didn't closely affect them was worrisome flippancy. Vera listened to her, although she looked at her email every once in a while to see if there was a message from Lisa. Viviana brought up the example of what happened in France with Charlie Hebdo: "The murder of journalists is unjustifiable," she said, "and making superficial comments aligned the posters, albeit naively, with the perpetrators of the massacre." Then, she leapt from Europe and the Middle East to Africa. Still upset, she went after Joseph Kony's army in Uganda and talked about the women who had had their breasts, lips, nose, ears, and feet amputated because they rode a bicycle. Obviously, Viviana had embraced this cause for some time, and she was not going to allow human idiocy to ruin it. A cause that had nothing to do with Vera but that she shared with her out of honor for their friendship. Viviana and Vera had known each other since graduate school. When Vera was starting, Viviana was finishing her doctorate. Viviana continued her harangue. Suddenly she asked Vera, without giving her time to respond: "Does naivete exist? Either they are terrifyingly immature, or they are true imbeciles," she almost immediately concluded. Vera had to go to class, but Viviana remained on the line, talking to her, without listening, talking to herself or to the receiver, to thin air, to her colleagues in California, to Mark Zuckerberg, to the president of the university. And suddenly, out of nowhere, she came out with: "Can you tell me how the humanities are going to be considered essential if we are represented by a bunch of idiots? Stop crying about the end of the humanities. Elevate your mission and don't become an onanistic highbrow group that feeds off its own subjective, confusing, and vague arguments." She said goodbye and hung up. Just like that, abruptly. Vera left quickly, not without checking the bags under her eyes. If the end of the humanities is coming, it's better to fix her image: her bags, her gray hairs, her disheveled mane. Don't let this be why they get rid of her, for being a misfit.

*Notebook*

She notes that her children made a video for their abuelo so she could send it to Lisa to show to her dad. Her children want to become scientists and find a cure for cancer. Her daughter also wants to save the elephants and her son the whales. Not to mention the trees: they're capable of lecturing anyone who abuses natural resources, especially about using paper. They're such gringos. Vera wonders what kind of parents they are and if they're leading their children in the right direction.

Day No Number

Lisa wrote her with the subject line *Progress!!!* She said that her father had asked her to bring him a pair of glasses. He'd told her that Dr. Casabilla came by and took out the tube from the wound and the one that went from his nose to his stomach. She couldn't say much more, but she'd write to them later and tell them about it. Vera and her brother responded with great enthusiasm and asked her to send a picture when possible.

*Notebook*

She doesn't know how to be a mother in Spanish, she writes. When she talks to her children, they answer her in English, and she immediately makes the switch, and her native tongue evaporates. She wasn't a mother in Buenos Aires, and therefore, her models were frozen in a time far away. Either she speaks like her parents spoke to her, or she speaks instantly translating from English to Spanish. Ever since they were young, she would sing them songs that her parents hummed to her, and she played all of María Elena Walsh's records so they would learn and listen to the good music from her country. But Argentina is a name for them, a point on a map in the southern hemisphere, another continent, in fact, since in school they teach them that there are seven continents, among them North America and South America. Argentina is such an abstract reality, and a little tangential, that they can idealize it in a way that only those who don't live there can. In her notebook she draws a house with a chimney and inside she poorly sketches people with dresses and bows on their heads, with hats and shorts, with suits and ties, with skirts and boots, like the little drawings she used to make when she was the same age as her daughter.

And later, on a separate page, she notes: Will they read *Dailan Kifki* in its original version?

Day No Number

Lisa writes them a WhatsApp with a note from their father that she transcribes on her phone:

> *My little chickadees: Lisa reads me every email that you send, and I really enjoy them. Unfortunately, there's no way I can answer them all, but each one you send me makes me very happy. Today, I have some news for you: for the first time, they offered me yogurt and applesauce. This is a big step for me, and I hope in the next few days I'll be able to have more food. Today, the surgeon stopped by personally and authorized all of this. That's all the important news I have for now. I feel your presence every day, and I love you all very much.*
>
> *Thanks a lot for the pictures and the little videos you're sending.*
>
> *Love,*
> DADDY

Vera read and reread the message many times over. She didn't know which part made her break down in tears. Was it that he called them "chickadees," was it that they had finally given him solid food, was it that he felt their presence all the time? Or was it everything all at once? Her sobs were profound, like from an unknown well deep inside. A sobbing that came and went like a gigantic wave destroying days, emotions, images. A wave that raises and displaces everything it finds in its path. It sinks into the well and comes out again even bigger and stronger. Victorious.

Vera and her brother wrote back, thrilled.

*Notebook*

A picture, she added in her notebook; I have to ask Lisa to send us a picture.

Day No Number

Vera got up, like always, at 6:30 A.M. She felt her way to the bathroom, and then she woke up her husband, her daughter, and her son. Still feeling her way around, she made it to the kitchen and turned on the burner. She needed coffee. The night before, she'd been up very late. She had called Lisa who had burst the bubble of happiness that she had blown up the day before. Perhaps that was Lisa's way of making her pay. The beginning of making her pay. Lisa told her that she had gotten to the hospital late . . .

. . . he was sleeping, and I woke him up. He

told me they had tortured him all afternoon . . . one doctor would leave and another one would come in. It was like that nonstop. They wouldn't give him a break. Just like when you both were here. His temperature is going up and down again, and the wound is infected. Besides, his glucose shoots up. I know that happens when there is an infection. That's why I went immediately to find the doctor on call. I asked him what was happening, and he told me that his white blood cells were a little high and that they must take action to localize the germ that's affecting him by taking cultures and treating him with an appropriate antibiotic . . . In the first culture, the germ was one usually found in the intestines . . . that's what the infectious disease specialist explained to me . . . but on Sunday, they took samples for another culture, and today, they took more . . . Yes, he is eating, and that is good, but he's not getting full. He's afraid . . . He got mad at me because he wanted me to bring him salt and flavored water . . . he told me that the nutritionist had authorized it . . . so I told him that I'd check . . . and he told me: I have to believe everything you say, and you don't believe anything I say! Logically, I checked. And, as usual, the nurses don't give him anything that is not written down, and one of them who heard about the flavored water explained to him that he is on an

> all-natural diet and that the water he was asking for has chemicals and preservatives that are not suitable for his health. He accepted it. I stayed to help him while he ate dinner . . . like at lunch. He ate that little tube pasta in broth with rice and some oil he added, but he left the sliced boiled carrots. For dessert he ate some pears with some sweetener he added . . . The day just goes on and on. He told me: I'm going backward . . . I put on my best face and tried to get him out of that hole by changing the subject. I don't feel like I can take care of things on my own, and I started asking him about things I needed to know so he would feel useful . . . he was perfectly lucid. Today they got him up, but he's just really scared . . . it was only to sit him in a chair . . . When I left, the nurse had already come to put him back to bed . . .

Vera hung up and turned off the phone. She could feel that Lisa was making her pay under the guise of a Good Samaritan. She got mad at Lisa because she wouldn't let him have flavored water or put salt on his food. But she didn't say anything. That was the price Vera paid for being far away. Getting mad from a distance could imply making her pay in another way, a way that could translate into a "why don't you come and take care of him yourself?" In the end, a humiliation. A slap in the face. She thought about her father and his inability to move by himself. About his fear and the loss of control over his own body. A body that now belonged to others. About Lisa and her power—now—over her father. A power she hadn't realized consciously, but in a certain way, she was manipulating. She thought again about her father. His body, it had no choice, it now belonged to the nurses, the surgeon, the doctors on duty, and above all, to Lisa.

*Notebook*

She notes: I feel so alienated that I can't think or feel. I am disconnected from the world but connected at the same time. This connection makes me feel out of place; it makes me numb. Being connected implies being committed to thousands of things at the same time. Thousands of things that strip me of feelings. They make me lose my sense of detail for the small and invisible things. For the things that really matter. I am an automaton. And then: When I go to the bathroom, I write secretly on my iPhone what I then transcribe here, in my notebook. With the excuse of "excusing" myself to go to the bathroom, I get my kids to give me five minutes of tranquility. When I come out, they follow me all around the house. They ask me for things, they present the arguments for or against something they're fighting about, they complain. I stop being a mother, a wife, a daughter, a writer, and I become a judge. My husband asks me about dinner, work, or the groceries. I can silence the iPhone so that if I'm typing, no one knows it. I'm like a teenager writing to a secret boyfriend. And when they call me—that is to say, when they yell for me or demand my inescapable presence—I legitimately justify myself and explain that I can't come out, I'm shitting, I'm peeing. It's a valid excuse. It's the excuse everyone can understand. In short, the bathroom is a mother's last refuge.

Day No Number

Vera asked Lisa to send her a picture of her father. Her brother did too. Lisa took advantage of this to tell them that she didn't think he was very happy. When she went to the hospital, he kept insisting that he had no strength. He tried to sit up in bed, and he could, with a little help from her. She added that fortunately, on the general care floor, the nurses weren't always on top of him like in intermediate care. She explained that he would doze for bits at a time, but he told her he couldn't sleep, and surely this was happening at night. She concluded that she had stayed until he finished lunch and that he had eaten less than half of what they'd served him. The kinesiologist came and made him do some exercises, and she specified that he had to keep doing them over and over. Lisa didn't know if he would do them on his own. Maybe if she were there, yes, but by himself . . . no . . . She added that she was going to take him a mirror so he could shave, and she was going to trim his nails. They'd grown like his beard and hair. He was going to dictate a message for them. We'd have to wait and see.

*Hi my little chickadees!*

*Luckily, I'm seeing some progress, and they've already switched me to another room.*

*They got me out of intermediate therapy. Really, you found out before me because you were in contact with the surgeon. They also took out the tube, and now I just have two or three IVs where they give me liquids and antibiotics. The kinesiologist is helping me regain my movement so I can walk. Today, I had full service because Lisa helped me shave and cut my fingernails. She even put some cologne on me. Lisa says that I look better now than I did this morning. They changed my menu, and I've been eating solid food for a couple of days now. When I have anything new to report, I'll send you a WhatsApp through Lisa.*

*I love you so, so, much, and I miss you.*

*Huge kisses to you all.*

*Daddy*

That night, Lisa sent a picture of her father to Vera and her brother.

*Notebook*

She notes: "They suck the aura from reality like water from a sinking ship."

Day No Number

Vera doesn't know what she will find when she opens the attachment, the picture Lisa took with her phone, the image of her father. Vera prefers a postponement. She confronts herself and confirms that she is a coward. Nothing about herself scares her anymore.

*Notebook*

She notes, laconically: I have nothing to write today. My mind is blank, and my words have dried up. In my heart there is sorrow and a bit of hope.

Day No Number

Vera probably avoided opening that email on purpose. They were planning a move, and she had a lot to do, between classes at the university and the tedium of putting everything in boxes. Nothing displeased her more. Such a lack of coordination. She didn't know if it was better to catalog all the objects and get rid of those she no longer needed, or to save time and pack everything indiscriminately. Postpone the agony and separate the wheat from the chaff, old clothes she no longer wore from the new stuff she'd never worn, the kids' clothes that no longer fit, the medicine that had expired, a few odd diapers and baby bottles that had fallen into disuse, portable baby bathtubs. And everything else, all that was still boxed up even before moving to this house, to the previous apartment, to the state where she lived, and even to the state before that: a violin that she had brought from her country, a violin that she liked as much or more than her father did, an instrument that she had gone with him to buy in the Flores neighborhood, when she envisioned herself as an indie and super cool electronic violinist. She let herself be pushed along by the rush of classes, meetings, work that had been waiting for days or months, boxes, motherhood, issues that come up at home and with the family. She answered emails and WhatsApps that Lisa and her brother sent, but every time her gaze landed on that email that she had not yet opened, Vera hesitated. So she postponed the encounter with the image of her father all shaved and cleaned up, according to how Lisa had described him. Proudly.

To say that Vera felt a stab in her stomach, a thousand stabs all over her body in unison, would not be right. It was like, together with the stabs, they had thrown buckets and buckets of cold water on her, like a gang of thugs had beaten her repeatedly and left her shattered, haggard, hollow on a dark street in an unknown city. A city in a strange country. Another world, another planet. Far away, in an unknown place. That's how she was for a while after she opened the attachment that was the picture of her father. How to explain that seeing his face that was trying to smile, wanting to show strength, pride in sitting up, losing weight and thin, so thin and in such a short time, so emaciated, so much like someone else that she couldn't establish a connection between the image that Lisa had sent and the image that she kept of him, that she always had. Vera left running and locked herself in the bathroom. Her refuge. She sat on the toilet seat and started to sob, with tears that came out like jets of water from a pressure hose while her children were beating on the locked door, crying, and asking if she was all right. She knew the lie about her contact lenses wouldn't work this time. What would she tell them? They, waiting, expectant, suffering from the unknown out of empathy from seeing their mother crying. She, split in two, between the instinctive necessity to guarantee them that everything was all right and her own suffering from seeing her father in such a deplorable state.

In five minutes, Vera was already back in the living-dining room, sitting at the table with her children, going between homework and dinner. She had no idea what had brought her to open that document in the afternoon when she was already in her role as mother, and not before, when her children were still at school. When her husband got home, she delegated her service and essential maternal role, escaped to her room, and got into bed. She wrapped herself inside of herself amid the sheets and the blankets, hiding her face and remembering, over and over again, her father's face. She slept more than usual. And each time she woke up she wondered about his fate. For the first time, she let her husband take care of preparing the kids' lunches, their clothes and breakfast for the next morning, and taking them to school. They would wear different colored socks, unwashed T-shirts, dress shoes instead of tennis shoes, or they would take the wrong food, but at least Vera would be able to rest and reflect on the future, if there was a long-term future with her father. And if there was one, how was or would that future be? How to intercede, to spy, to understand what was now presenting itself as a uniform and vast mass, as a horizontal line that ended in an infinitesimal dot. And on the way toward that open slit, infinite sequences and images blurred with what was, will be, could be, and could have been.

*Notebook*

She writes, mentally, a quote from María Zambrano: "An image can never be entirely diaphanous without the threat of it being erased. It can be that way, it can even dissolve itself, and then, whatever it was carrying, its emotive charge, gets diminished in the medium of vision, gets coated, and can, on its own, tinge all content, the entire field of reality." She notes: When she uses the verb *diminish,* is she referring to "to dilute" or "to become undone"? She writes the image of her father. What is it like to write the image of her father? She does not write "the image of her father," nor does she draw it; rather, she writes the image. Yes, she writes, edits, pinpoints the image in such a way that few, very few, know how to write, edit, and pinpoint. To write the image of her father is to loan words to that configuration of chromatic lines that, blurred and wrinkled, imprints itself against the cortex of her memory.

Day No Number

The biopsy. Vera asked about the results of the biopsy. She also talked to a doctor friend of hers from Panama and asked if he would read the report once she received it. No matter what Dr. Casabilla thought, she wanted a second opinion. She wrote to Lisa and asked how her father had made it through the night. Lisa responded laconically, *I'll write you a little later.* Vera felt Lisa's power over the situation, the way she created expectations to then topple them in one breath. Her phone vibrated again, and, although Vera was driving to the university to teach, she grabbed it. She waited until she stopped at a light to read it:

> *He's feeling down again and drowsy. It looks like he had a bad night. He's not getting his strength back very easily. Also, there's a problem with his bowel movements . . . he feels like going all of a sudden, and he can't make it to the portable toilet they put by his bed. I asked the doctor on duty, and he told me the digestive tract had changed . . . but with time they'd be giving him medication for that. You can just imagine the situation: portable toilet, portable urinal, and now a walker . . . That's what the kinesiologist brought to see if he could use it a little this afternoon.*
>
> *It's just so sad! I hope he can rest. I've been here since midmorning, and I'll leave him tucked in after dinner. Tomorrow, Sunday, I'll do the same . . . he won't be alone. xoxo.*

The horn from the car behind her jarred her back to reality. She shot out into traffic and almost hit another car that had cut in front of her without signaling. Outside her office, three students were waiting anxiously to go over their grades. She was late, the same as she had been for the last few days, and the coordinator of the department had left a note on her door warning the students that she might be delayed. One of the students had eaten lunch with her the week before. The lunch had consisted of a meeting for undergraduate students whose major, or at least one of the many majors that they usually pick, was Latin American Studies. They had gotten together in one of the oldest and most picturesque mansions on campus where, every day at noon, they hashed out academic projects of all kinds. The student who was waiting at her office door had done a presentation on her thesis project: a comparative perspective of public education in countries like Argentina and Cuba. To do this, besides Paulo Freire, she was using sources like Enrique Dussel and Walter Mignolo. She was considering the coloniality of knowledge and the "Global South" versus the "North" with that naivete and haughtiness that only students from the United States can have. Argentine arrogance is different, Vera thought to herself. Arrogance in Argentina is I know everything, I mix in everything, ergo I'm a genius. It's a top-down way of looking at the world in an often baseless and superior way, also naive. But an inductive naivete. Arrogance in the United States was different and implied looking at things in an opposing way: from bottom up, accompanied by a naivete that the students themselves are not aware of, and in a certain way, deductive. A naivete that does not lead them to think they know everything, but that each idea they apprehend encompasses a totality. A totality that does not know there is more, because of ignorance. A truncated, fragmented totality. A counter-totality. At lunch, while the student was describing her project and possible arguments, Vera felt that she, the student, was turning into a product of the coloniality of knowledge. She didn't tell her, nor did she want to embarrass her publicly. To the contrary, she congratulated her. But that afternoon, back in her office, she was no longer thinking about the coloniality of knowledge. She was thinking about biopolitics and how her father's body was caught at the intersection of other dominions and sovereignties. She began to again feel how Lisa was making them pay from afar. And she reflected on the path the debilitation had taken on all the organs that made up the person who was her father. About the distinction between person and body. Between the material and the symbolic. When the student, who was waiting outside with the others, came into her office and asked her what she thought about the essay she had sent her after lunch the week before, Vera said "excellent" and pushed her back to the hallway. She apologized to the other students who were waiting to see her and asked them to please come back later. She closed the door, turned off the light, and sat with her eyes closed tightly, facing the window. She might have even fallen asleep.

*Notebook*

She paraphrased in her notebook what Lisa had said that afternoon: her father still cannot leave the hospital.

He's not well enough. First, he must conquer his fear and begin to get out of bed. He's got to start moving. If he doesn't move, they're not going to release him. She talked to Dr. Casabilla, who also detected his fear. He's got to gradually take a few steps with the walker, he said, with or without the kinesiologist. He's got to get to the bathroom to brush his teeth. He doesn't need to worry about the problem with his bowel movements that come so suddenly but think more about the progress he's making. Lisa talked to her father about this, and they made a deal that the next day he would get his act together because, otherwise, he would keep getting weaker. She was going to be more energetic. To bring him home, at a minimum, he would have to walk holding on to the walls. She got some strength from who knows where and really let him have it. She scolded him like a child. She told him to really think about what they had said and that if he doesn't follow her advice he's going to have to stay and live in the hospital. That she is worn out. And that she hopes to get the biopsy toward the end of the week.

Day No Number

Vera tried again to return to the novel she had wanted to write before her father got sick. It was now flickering on a horizon of possibilities and uncertainties. A little light that twinkled inconsistently. But there was no story in that conglomeration of words. There was no plot. There were no characters. The text lying in front of her with an inexact title consisted of loose puzzle pieces. Notes she jotted down months ago took another direction after she found herself in the hospital, the one where her father was admitted: hasty reflections on her time spent in Buenos Aires, on when she stayed at her mother's house; considerations that accumulated in the moments when she wasn't hijacked by the ideas and emotions that besieged her daily, or by the frozen image of her father after surgery. That image of a plastic dummy she had to exchange for another to free herself, only to disappear again afterwards, when Lisa sent Vera and her brother the image of her father in the hospital all cleaned up and shaved, an image that upset her even more and left her submerged in a sort of somniferous delirium. The novel, or text, that Vera was trying to write was made up of hallucinations she would scribble in her iPhone when she would awake violently at three in the morning with an urgent need to edit, to put words into a sequence of images and thoughts that both cleared her head in the middle of the night and stalked her, like the stealthy eyes of crocodiles at night, those eyes she had identified in her kids' nature magazine and that now reappeared in the form of a premonition. Notes that filtered through her computer between classes and emails, between readings and meetings and maternal responsibilities; drafts of sentences and phrases that she mentally wrote when she didn't have anything to write with at hand, when her creativity was on sabbatical, on pause, and then she would again take up her daily activities.

*Notebook*

She writes: Why is she seduced so much by dreaming about herself as a famous writer? Not as a movie star, not as a politician, not as a businesswoman, not as a housewife, not as a rock singer. No, simply as a famous writer who is asked to give talks and tours all over the world to talk about her characters (they're missing: she writes without characters), about her writing process (none: she writes desperately in the bathroom, excusing herself every time, saying she's peeing or shitting), about her imagination (she lacks one: it's like a game of ping-pong that goes back and forth, it compulsively splits up and becomes paralyzed), about her childhood (now she dreams up a genealogy, a typical lie for all writers: She read Proust when she was seven, in French! She read Faulkner and Poe when she was eight, in English! And she read Cervantes' Quixote when she was nine, in Castilian Spanish!), about her adulthood, which implies being a mother and a writer (craziness!), about what is implied by being a writer and working as a professor in academia in the United States (schizophrenia!), about what is implied by being a writer and a critic in the United States and writing in Spanish (self-boycott! Because for us, she explains imaginarily in one of those book tours in gorgeous libraries with idiotic and nonexistent readers, for us, everything is hashed out in situ. If you're not there lobbying with fellow writers from your country, you don't exist. You are nothing, you are done. Even though you never became anyone).

Day No Number

That morning, after leaving the kids at school, Vera and her husband devoted themselves to emptying dressers and closets and putting all the contents into boxes. Once they were filled, they put a tag on each box with a vague description of what was inside and sealed them with heavy-duty tape. When she sat down to rest and have a glass of water, she saw that her phone lit up, and, when she grabbed it, she saw immediately that it was Lisa:

> *Big progress! When I got there this morning he was walking with the kinesiologist and then he walked without the walker. He also made it to the bathroom to pee with the walker, and I followed him because he's still not very stable. They've taken away the IV fluids and the antibiotic since the infectious disease doctor had already told me that the cultures were okay or that the antibiotic had a positive effect. He's already taken his first pill! He's speaking better, and he just went by himself to sit on the toilet in the bathroom!!! All this gives him a lot of confidence. He told me that the infectious disease doctor came by the room when I wasn't there, and she began to explain to him how they had removed his spleen . . . his eyes filled with tears . . . So he told me . . . she explained that when they take out the spleen, you have to bear in mind that you lack defenses, and you have to get protection from disease through vaccines. Once a year or every two*

*years. And that another infectious disease doctor will have to follow his case. She didn't talk to him about the other organs, but your dad told me that when she started to go into detail . . . he preferred for her to explain it all to me. He seemed really sad when he was telling me. xoxo.*

Vera thought again about her father's right to know and why she, her brother, and Lisa had decided to obey the directives of Dr. Casabilla. Why they hadn't refused to follow his suggestions, and why unanimously they decided not to tell her father what he was going through, what happened during surgery, and what they had removed. She had discussed this with some of her friends who were doctors in the United States, and without fail, they looked at her with surprise. They explained that by law all patients have the right to know about their illness, and it was not ethical to hide it from them. Vera thought Dr. Casabilla's attitude could be paternalistic, and his paternalism was a quintessentially Latin American problem. In the northern hemisphere, due to different laws (laws that shaped culture), they looked at her like she was from another planet. Nonetheless, Vera agreed that her father should be told about what he was going through. Either she had become Americanized and was thinking like a gringa, or something deep inside was provoking an unbearable empathy. She wrote to Lisa and her brother. She told them what she was thinking and asked for Lisa to talk to him and tell him. Her brother was the first to disagree. It didn't even take five minutes for him to reply. Her father was weak, and there had been a survey that showed a certain tendency: patients who did not know what they were suffering from recovered faster than those who knew. Lisa intervened and added that her father was in no condition to know what he had. That information could be fatal. And you think he doesn't suspect? Vera asked. They're treating him like a child, but he isn't. He's seventy-three years old. Lisa threw that option out, making her pay even more, since Vera felt useless and overruled, lacking access to her father, not being able to talk to him or explain what she was thinking or feeling. Her words were being intercepted since it was Lisa who wrote and transcribed what the doctors were saying, editing what was better to take out or leave in and changing the content she thought would better favor her position in the face of the misfortune her father was suffering. The mediator was now beginning to take vengeance upon her father, the object of the dispute, who slowly was losing more control not only over his body, his destiny, and his fate, but also over what he knew and what he didn't know. At seventy-three years old, her father, Vera's father, had been dismissed and reduced to a childlike state. His authority to decide on his own behalf had been stripped away just like they had stripped away his organs, and he had succumbed to the power of the woman he lived with, his children, the doctors, the nurses. They had built a stage set around him and hidden the true nature of what he had and what he had started to become.

*Notebook*

She found that one day she had noted in her iPhone the following platitude: "Don't expect anything from anyone and you'll never be disappointed." And she wrote, then, much later, when she stumbled on this cliché that her magnificent wisdom had given her. Why should I have to expect anything from Lisa? Lisa is not my mother; she can't make me pay what my mother would if she were in her place (she can't oblige me to go back through guilty insinuations or deep psychopathological blows, like those that cut to the deepest part of my marrow), but for the same reason, she can betray me even more. Lisa, poor Lisa, immolated Lisa, the nighttime avenger returns, a representative—without knowing it—of that coloniality of knowledge that her students so enjoyed repeating and abusing, without even understanding to what they were referring. Lisa, colonizer and imperialist. Who would have thought it?

Day No Number

They finally told her they were going to release her father. Lisa wrote to let her know that there had been *zero news* from Dr. Casabilla, but the doctor on duty had said that it was possible for him to get out in very few days. Most probably on the weekend. Vera knew her father was half-hearted despite having made progress and taking short walks down the hospital hallway with his kinesiologist. She also knew, through Lisa, that he had made it to the bathroom on time, no problem, but he needed more self-confidence and to cheer up. Besides this, she found out that he couldn't speak. His voice wasn't sounding like it always had, his voice had become strange, and he'd lose it after just trying to say two or three words.

*Dear chickadees:*

*Good news! Surely by this weekend I'll be home again. It's not a definite release yet. A nurse will come to the house to continue with wound care and a kinesiologist to help strengthen my muscles. And according to what they told us, a clinician will come by two times a week to make sure everything's under control.*

*We'll keep you informed about my progress.*

*Lots of kisses to everyone.*

*I love you very much.*

*See you soon.*

*Daddy*

As soon as they received this WhatsApp written by Lisa but dictated by her father, her brother wrote to Dr. Casabilla asking about the results of the biopsy and when the oncologist would become part of the treatment plan. He wanted to know if their father already had an assigned specialist or if they needed to look for one, if he had any suggestion or recommendation. He also asked "how the flow of information would be handled" with Vera's father (and his father), considering that "little by little he is finding out about his situation due to the different doctors who are visiting him," and that, without knowing the strategy imposed by Dr. Casabilla, certain fragments of his diagnosis are filtering through little by little . . . He then closed, wishing him kind regards accompanied by a "Have a good weekend." He didn't respond to that that message. Since it was summer in Argentina, January to be specific, Dr. Casabilla was probably spending the summer in Pinamar or Punta del Este. Or the United States. Visiting old friends in Pittsburgh. Or in Europe, with his children and grandchildren. Lisa wrote him again, since the doctor on duty had explained to her that Vera's father must go to the surgeon (Dr. Casabilla) for a follow-up after he had been released. He shouldn't wait more than a week. Vera wrote him another email. This time he responded.

> Dear Vera,
>
> It is essential that I see your father for an evaluation, from a clinical-surgical perspective, of his postoperative and postrelease progress. This is apart from the anatomic pathology.
>
> During the month of January, I will be seeing patients on Mondays. I believe that the day after tomorrow is too soon to see your father, and it will exhaust him too much to bring him to my office. Therefore, I hope to see him the following Monday, one week after his release. By that time,

the report with the results of the biopsy will most likely be available.

Please tell Lisa to confirm the schedule for his visit with my secretary Constanza.

Sincerely,
DR. J. CASABILLA

How many patients had passed under the eyes of Dr. Casabilla? How many had survived and how many had disappeared? Vanished into whatever may come, ceasing to exist. Vera knew she couldn't understand the concept of disappearing. Rationally, she could, but not in existential terms. And was the existential perhaps less rational or not rational? Maybe she was confusing the categories of analysis. What she did know, without a doubt, was that she could never be as immune as the doctors, who saw their patients go from an arrogant strength to a pitiful fragility. It was the slowness in the extinction of a life that was so hard for her to understand. A paradoxical slowness because that latent extinction would nevertheless appear at any moment, suddenly, like it appeared in her father, taking with it a constellation of memories. A continuous series of moments that would evaporate, that would cease to exist forever. She would not be able to understand it. She knew it. Because it is as if a star were going out, or thousands of radiant spheres, a light in the darkness while two stealthy eyes wait, patient or expectant, like crocodiles at night.

*Notebook*

She notes that what she thinks and writes has metamorphosed and become a single membrane. She points out that she'd been happy for the last few days after she had received the news of his release. But she also writes that she'd found herself disoriented. And she still was unable to assimilate the image of her father in the hospital. The image Lisa, happy, had sent. The image that she digitally celebrated, through emails and WhatsApps. A false celebration, of course, because in that image she read his face, his eyes that couldn't look directly at the camera, disoriented in a semi-vertical position that had possibly been forced. She writes that the move had thrown her out of place. While she thinks about her father getting out of the hospital, she realizes that she also has to pack up, get her suitcases ready, fill boxes and boxes until she empties what is full and turns it over to the highest bidder. Save and throw away. Go through old photos, notes, folders, papers. Catalog. Put stickers with big red letters according to spatial categories: kids' room, kitchen, bathrooms, fragile (really big and in all caps because movers are like robots or what's left of lobotomized people; they say yes to everything, but they don't think, they don't calculate, they don't even imagine. They pick up, move, and deposit. Welcome to Corporate America!).

Day No Number

For some reason Vera cried when she looked at the pictures of her children that she was sending to Buenos

Aires so her father could see them and cheer up. Not because of the pictures alone, but because they are images loaded with intentionality. Pictures that have an additional element that one can't see but feel, touch: portraits whose mission is a) to show her father they are thinking about him often; b) to cheer her father up with the presence—albeit virtual—of his grandchildren; c) to insert her father into daily life.

*Notebook*

She writes about Maury, the lady who helps her clean her house. She writes that having a person to help her is difficult because she's put in a situation where she's telling Maury what to do and how she should do it. It's as if suddenly, in the blink of an eye, she had become her own mother. She doesn't know what happened or how time had passed so quickly, but there she was, saying this, that, and the other to this lady. She notes: Maury is nice, and I smile at her, but she doesn't listen to me when I talk to her. She agrees all the time. I speak to her in Spanish. Nonetheless, she didn't write this, because it seemed taboo to say it: at times, when she looked at her, she felt disgust. Despite her being nice and cordial, there was something in her that inspired a certain aversion. Almost repugnance. The same sensation she had when, at the university, she would see a colleague, a professor in the French Literature Department, drinking from the water fountain. She noted: Is it that her open lips make the shape of a dead fish? Is it her lack of academic rigor, her willingness to carry on as a little old language teacher and not as a researcher? Maury is also a teacher. She was, really, when she lived in Mexico. Northern Mexico. How strange. My mother was also a teacher.

Day No Number

Lisa told them she had the results of the biopsy. She had picked them up that morning. She took a picture of them with her phone and sent it to them. Vera read the description, divided into macroscopic and microscopic detail. It was a histopathological report. Vera realized her limitations in understanding what exactly had occurred inside her father's body. And, more than anything, what his fate would be, if he'd have a fate, if he'd play tennis again, if he'd travel to see her, to see them, to meet up with everyone in Miami. She read that the "proliferation index evaluated by means of the Ki-67 technique (MIB-1) is 4%," but she couldn't figure out what that percentage meant. On the Internet she found the following information: Ki-67 is a "cellular marker for proliferation" and the "pathologist determines the proliferation index of cancer cells under the microscope." According to the web page, it's a measure that determines the speed of growth of a tumor, and the higher the Ki-67 proliferation index, the faster the cells are dividing. She kept reading till the end where it said: "determinations ≥10 would indicate an adverse prognosis."

If thirty is high, then four is low. That was her first conclusion. And, in a certain way, she even felt happy. But then, why did she decide to write to Dr. Casabilla again? Why did she send the pictures that Lisa had taken of the report asking him for an immediate diagnosis? Why did she insist that he be "as clear and transparent as possible" and that he explain it, since she, like her brother, living outside the country, had to organize things in order to be with their father in Buenos Aires should it be necessary in the coming months?

> Dear Vera,
>
> This is advanced cancer of the pancreas. The prognosis, in general terms, is not good. He is still too weak to handle possible chemotherapy treatments.
>
> Let's hope that his general state improves, although he is much better than when you both left.
>
> Patience.
>
> JC

*Notebook*

"The prognosis is not good," she writes. And she adds, "The higher the Ki-67 proliferation index, the faster the cells are dividing." While she's scribbling in her notebook, it's probably not registering that her father is suffering from metastatic pancreatic cancer. She's denying it, delaying it, or evading it. Therefore, she notes that living far from her parents is hell. *Latitude Penance,* that should be the title of her novel. Of her fragmented text, like shards of a mirror, broken and invisible. Fragments she will never regain because the past with her father remains suspended in a capsule. If she could only digest it. Regain what is slowly draining from her life. Not *Imperfect Present.* Not *The Devoured One.* Not *The Devouring Imperfect Present.* Living far away, growing old far away. Shards and more shards.

Day No Number

Vera told Lisa she'd call her father that afternoon, after class. Lisa asked her not to talk long because he tired easily. Once again, Lisa was taking control of her father's time, and she handed it out according to her own criteria. It was probably another way she would have to pay for being far away. She called him that afternoon, as she had promised. Her father answered immediately. Vera noticed that he perked up and made an additional effort to show that he was okay. At first his voice sounded happy, but almost immediately, just as Lisa had predicted, his voice began to grow faint. She felt the fatigue and unease despite the distance and cell phone communication. She perceived an instantaneous depletion. Her father quickly became exhausted and was left without energy, like a deflated ball. Vera talked to him and told him not to talk any more. She told him all the news; she talked about her move preparations. She said to herself that she was sorry she wasn't there to take his hand and hold it tightly. To give him a big smile, so big that it would engulf him. Despite her efforts to dominate the dialogue, her father tried to tell her about his feat of the day: walking to the kitchen with his walker, eating cherry gelatin, and going to the bathroom alone. Vera got herself together and encouraged him (she also deflated as she listened closely from the other side of the receiver). She congratulated him like a child. She congratulated him in Spanish—mentally translating from English—because that was the language that stuck in her palate every day, and she didn't spit it out, because it was also a language of affection. Good job, Dad, she thought in English. When she hung up, she saw how long the call had lasted: three minutes and forty-eight seconds.

*Notebook*

Why can't she write in her yellow-paged notebook about the picture that Lisa sent her? Is it the deterioration, the degradation of his body, his face, unrecognizable, even when she could find his gaze within those eyes, his hair in that confused, white tangle that surrounded him like a golden glow. Her inability to describe what she had felt bothered her deeply. But is description necessary in order to feel? Does one feel even if one doesn't put words to those impressions that hit like a whip or rapid machine gun fire? Perhaps she should give up. Perhaps she should keep that feeling, treasure it. Perhaps that feeling was not something to be conjured up with words, but, to the contrary, she should preserve it. A memory that would live in her as a testimony of a lost battle, never begun. Who said that one must take impressions out and give them forms through art, whether with words or other aesthetic resources? Perhaps the image would come out on its own, in its time, naturally or transformed into something different. Or perhaps it would remain filed away in a corner of her heart, terrified and trembling, apprehensive to come out and become matter.

Day No Number

The move took place the day after her daughter's birthday. With so much stress, they couldn't organize a party. Her daughter reproached them for it, but Vera convinced her that the trip to Disney World with her other grandfather, the one from the United States—and the one they'd take with the whole family in a few short weeks—was just as good as or better than a birthday party. That convinced her daughter, and therefore, Vera and her husband could fully surrender to the exhaustion and tension that moving implied. For one whole day they watched people lifting furniture and boxes, loading them on a huge truck, unloading them, and depositing them into the new house. But the new house was an old house they had decided to renovate, and because of the habitual construction delays, it wasn't ready. This added anxiety to the process of changing homes. And Vera, even if she was distracted and stopped thinking about her father's illness, became more anguished. The house was under construction, in medias res, unfinished. She thought about her children, about the loose nails still scattered around, about the smell of paint, and about the workers who would come back to the house with all of them living there to hammer, fix, put things in and pull things out, make holes and then patch them, align closets and cabinets, and seal moldings.

Day No Number

From her office, Vera sent a WhatsApp to Lisa, who would finally go with her father to see Dr. Casabilla. It was his first visit since they released him from the hospital. Lisa responded flustered and asked her, as well as her brother, to be patient. Vera thought that everyone was asking for patience. She went to teach, and when she got back to her office, she read:

> *We're in the waiting room. There's a lot of people. After this I'm going home, we'll eat lunch, and I'll go to the store. I'll write you from there. I'm not going to stop writing you. I never have, and I've never kept anything from you. I'm only asking for a little time. Your father is losing his balance quite a bit. In the last three days he fell three times at home.*

And right after that, she found the following:

> *I just got to the store. Casabilla paid more attention to the low glucose. He said that he could die from that and remain unconscious in a diabetic coma. He*

*looked at me as if to say . . . you're the one who's taking care of him. I told him: "Doctor, I'm not neglecting him, it's just that he used to control this on his own, and now I'm having to help him." Your daddy is weak, and the doctor realized it. He asked him if he's eating . . . and even if he is, he gets full quick, and really, nothing else is happening. He gave us some enzymes, tablets for before lunch and dinner. Then he asked me for the pathological report, and he explained to him, "Your children want me to speak with you now because, up until this point, we had wanted you to have time to recover from the surgery, which took place exactly two months ago." He explained to him that what he had at the moment prior to the operation was a malignant tumor in the pancreas and another one above the stomach, and that the treatment he must continue with now is oncological, but that he was still not in condition to receive any treatment. It was better to wait two weeks and give him a little more time to recuperate. Your daddy was nervous. When we left, Casabilla ran into us in the street, and even though I always have him by the hand, he tripped and almost fell . . . He told him that tripping could be very dangerous, that he could break a bone . . . he recommended that he use a cane. So, he got even more nervous, and words just wouldn't come out of his mouth. I told Casabilla I was afraid he was anemic, so he said he'd ask his secretary to order a full analysis and also ask for the tumor marker . . . If he doesn't get up to eat something sweet tonight, I'll take him to have the blood work done tomorrow. When we were going home, I didn't want to stress that the tumor was malignant . . . I just talked about the tumor. I told him that, knowing you both were fully aware, I had consulted an oncologist about the results of the biopsy, and she told me that chemotherapy treatment was an option when it was necessary and when the patient was strong enough. "And why the oncologist?" he says to me . . . I answered because it is the specialty that is devoted to the treatment of tumors. "I'm not going to go to an oncologist . . . if the treatment is aggressive . . . I don't want it." We didn't have much more time to talk . . . I didn't want to dig any deeper either because his eyes were already filling up with tears . . . Was I clear? We now have an appointment on Monday at 9:00 A.M, the same time as today. I just feel like shit. xoxo.*

*Notebook*

She writes in her yellow notebook that ever since she moved to the new house, she has turned into a brick. A tile, a paving stone, a piece of ceramic. Plaster. Cement, sand, drywall. She notes that her world, since the move, has been getting smaller and was making her smaller. She is now domestic. She has become just what she always detested: the consummate housewife. Now I fluctuate between the granite kitchen counters, the couch filled with dust, the toilet seat you have to change because it's broken, the housekeeper who comes late or doesn't come at all, wineglasses and dishes in boxes, the oven, sheets, paint drips the workers leave on the windows, wooden floors, plumbers who explain in Spanglish that the "pipa" in the kids' bathroom is "leakiando," the arrogant construction boss who does things his own way, poorly and in a hurry. She says to herself that ever since she moved, there have been nothing but horrible days. She thinks about what she's been eating: pure junk. Supposedly healthy cereal bars, even though they're filled with sugar; a gigantic sandwich that she devoured in five minutes while the workers "cleaned" the chaos they had just left in the kitchen and while she was running out to pick up the kids from school. Potato chips, snap peas, all the food her son didn't eat at school and returned intact in his lunch box, a lot of wine (to dull the pain, the anxiety, the stress), raw bell peppers, and an orange. She concludes: I'm surrounded by boxes, incapable of finding what I need, incapable of helping my kids with their homework. Pure boxes and people who work here inside the house, they fix what still needs to be fixed, they listen to a radio show about unthinkable sexual fantasies in Mexican Spanish. Their world is so different from mine. I fluctuate between the BBC and NPR. And, nonetheless, they don't even notice. They don't notice the radio's commercials that come between rancheras that hammer at your brain. I'm the only one who notices; the blaring radio continues, but none of them feel the need to censure what's being heard like I do. More than censorship, it's shame. Shame, being ashamed for them, or, who knows, maybe ashamed of myself.

Day No Number

Vera was paralyzed. A new WhatsApp from Lisa left her speechless. *Night's coming. Hard times are on their way.*

*Notebook*

She writes: Refrigerator full, washer empty. A house full of boxes; workers who are captivated by their cell phones, who spy out of the corners of their eyes, with sidelong glances. The boss comes in, gives an order, and disappears into the labyrinth of empty rooms. She doesn't jot it down, but she wonders when she will unpack, when will she take the contents out of the boxes, so they stop being a wall that surrounds her and turn into a feasible materiality. Meanwhile, her children hide in them and make cardboard forts. They hide out and come out laughing; they drag themselves around inside the boxes from one place to another, leaving the packaging full of transparent bubbles all over the house, leaving paths and codes she doesn't pay much attention to or even try to decipher.

Day No Number

Lisa writes:

> *Last night he told me, "Is it so serious that my*

*kids have to come so often?" I told him that your brother had some vacation days saved up and that you wanted to spend more time with him, since when you were here, he was still in the ICU. He didn't believe me. He talked about how much it would cost you, your brother, the kids, and school.*

And then:

*He's not eating very much. He had a piece of toast for breakfast and a piece of chicken for lunch, and nothing to go with it. If he'd had his way, he would've skipped lunch. Now he's gone to lie down. Everything's weighing heavy on him. According to his blood work, his cholesterol is typical of someone who's malnourished, the clinician told me. She told your dad: You have to eat because if not, I'll have to put in a nasogastric tube . . . On Tuesday, they're bringing some medicine to boost his appetite . . . I hope it works. And also, some protein powder to sprinkle on top of his food.*

Vera opens a magazine from her university where they're announcing funds for a program called Medical Humanities. She reads that her colleague, who directs the program and is also her friend, says that "although we know, in the medical humanities, that the human experience of illness does not equal numeric values that are written in the patient's chart, we also know that the experience of human illness cannot be reduced to quantitative data and digital signals." She wonders how her colleague-friend would include the human part in the medical history, how she would extract the human part of the data that keeps us from trying new techniques in the field of medical assistance. Vera thinks her translation is generous. She thinks about her father, about the quantitative data and the experience of illness crashing together. She thinks about his slow debilitation. About her conversations that last no longer than three minutes.

How to extract what is human from the medical odyssey. Maybe by writing.

*Notebook*

She writes: Is this perhaps the end of the world of words? I long for a world of music.

Day No Number

The day before she left for Disney World, Vera packed her bags and went out for a run. She needed to clear her mind. She felt bewildered. The trip had been planned for more than six months. Her father-in-law had planned it so he could see her kids. She would go first, and her husband would join them in Orlando, after he finished his classes at the university. That same day Lisa wrote to her to tell her that she had called the ambulance. Vera had finished her run, and now she was pacing and running around the house in circles. First, she saw that Lisa had said that the kinesiologist had just left and told her that her father was going to start getting weaker and weaker. He was lying down now, and she was going out to get him some dried fruit. He was overcome with anxiety. She asked if she could write to Casabilla to show him the most recent blood work. Their next appointment was not for another week, and she didn't want to wait. Then she told her that the ambulance had come, but in the end, they had not taken him. Vera's heart stopped. The doctor had ordered specific blood and urine tests, and the numbers were all good. Vera started breathing again. She went into her house, opened the suitcases, threw in what she found at hand without thinking about what she needed. She ignored the workers who were patching and fixing holes, sanding walls, and sawing wood outside; they were yelling at each other in a language that, although clearly recognizable, was not hers. She locked herself in the bathroom, shielded from all the glances. Then sadness came out like a torrent.

*Notebook*

To write grief. To write degradation. To chronicle those steps that illness takes to prey on its victims. To honor the victim describing the penance. A penance that robs a person's will. That takes away everything.

Day No Number

When Vera landed in Orlando, she turned on her

phone. Lisa told them that he was inside the ambulance, en route to the hospital. She had noticed her father had some type of imbalance; he was shaking and talking nonsense. Completely disoriented. She had called the doctor who decided to admit him to see what was happening. When she had any news, she would let them know. Vera got off the plane. Her children happily ran to see her father-in-law. Nothing could be more fun than being at Disney World. With a forced smile, Vera retrieved the luggage and headed for the resort hotel with her father-in-law, his partner, and her kids. Vera noticed that images of Mickey and Minnie smiling were everywhere. All around her were smiles and dreams coming true. The world of fantasy was overpowering her, and she, with her hands and feet tied, could not set herself free.

*Notebook*

She notes: My words have dried up.

Day No Number

Early that morning, Vera bought a ticket to go to Buenos Aires at the end of the month. Then she went with the kids to breakfast, and after that, everyone got on the shuttle that would take them to Magic Kingdom. The kids were jumping all around, and Vera, between rides, was trying to keep up with her messages:

Lisa: We're in one of the rooms in the on-call unit at

the hospital. I started the paperwork . . . chest x-ray, labs, and admissions.

Brother: Is he awake?

Lisa: Yes . . . but he's dozing . . . he doesn't have any strength . . . maybe these are signs of dehydration.

Brother: Do you think we should contact Casabilla?

Lisa: I don't know. I'm desperate. He doesn't even know where he is. I want to think it's only because he's dehydrated. He's calm . . . but while we were coming in the ambulance, he was saying . . . when did the train pass . . . you forgot your keys . . . at least I told you . . .

Brother: Just be calm, Lisa. He's probably just had an imbalance. No better place than there to get him under control. Did the doctors say anything?

Lisa: Yes, they just started his blood work . . . they still have to do the x-ray . . . It looks like Vera still hasn't read anything!

Vera read the message exchange when she got off one of the rides: Pirates of the Caribbean. The sound of the speakers announcing the next parade, plus the screams of the children and their parents jumping up and down, asking to go see the characters who were close by and waving and taking pictures with them, next to lines and lines of people everywhere, everything kept her from organizing her thoughts. Or better yet, it kept her from thinking. She wrote to Lisa asking her to take her father's hand and hold it tight. To whisper in his ear how much she missed him. Lisa told them that the nurse had come to do the EKG and hang the IV to hydrate him. Then they took him for a chest x-ray. After that, they will admit him.

*Notebook*

She notes: Is it necessary to poke and prod him and take blood, roll him from one room to another under an intense, white light, with people he doesn't know who talk to him in technical jargon?

Day No Number

Vera woke up to the sound of messages. Lisa said:

> *I spoke with the doctor. He doesn't think he'll make it until when you've planned to come. His abdomen is full of liquid. For now, they're not going to puncture it, unless it begins to press on the lungs and he can't breathe. He's already in renal failure. They're not feeding him . . . it makes no sense. With this kind of tumor . . . since they diagnosed it . . . they don't live more than six months, and unfortunately . . . we're at that limit. He already told me he's not going to get better and for me to tell you that he loves you very much. I feel like shit.*

Vera did not read what the words were saying. She did not see the meaning, only the form. Her children were running from one place to another, and she was feigning a smile, regretting that she couldn't lock herself in the bathroom and sob openly. Her husband had not yet arrived, and she couldn't leave Disney World. She wanted to get on an airplane and land in Buenos Aires. She didn't even have her passport.

She wrote to Lisa that she would change her flight to go in two or three days, depending on what she could get. How's he doing? *He drifts in and out of sleep, and his skin is so sensitive that he can't even tolerate when they take his blood pressure. Even with a catheter, he can't urinate . . . they've just hung a diuretic drip.*

Vera and her brother insisted on no invasive procedures.

*Notebook*

A world without words, what would that be like?

Day No Number

Vera got up and went with her kids to breakfast. Today, they would go to Tomorrowland. Her phone wasn't working well. She didn't see the following dialogue:

Brother: Lisa, any news?

Lisa: He's in palliative care . . . with morphine and subcutaneous analgesics. Nothing invasive, and it would seem like there is an infection but no fever. I'm not moving from here.

Brother: Is he conscious?

Lisa: He's sleeping and wakes up from time to time. He's on oxygen.

She writes to Lisa that she'll only be able to get a plane out on Monday since she had to go get her passport. She is worried.

Lisa: Things here are not going well at all, and I can't talk.

Vera: But is he conscious? When we talked yesterday, he was. I understand you can't talk, but write me, because it's so painful when I'm so far away, and I can't see what you see.

Lisa: Vera . . . I understand, but I'm not moving from this room. He's in palliative care, morphine, analgesics. He moves from one side to the other. Nothing aggressive, but I don't know how long we have. That's the reality.

Vera: But is he conscious?

Lisa: He responds sometimes.

Vera: Please, Lisa, tell my dad that I'll be there on Tuesday. To please wait for me. Tell him when he's conscious to please wait for me, that I want to see him.

*Notebook*

She writes: I was sitting in one of those little tram cars that take you through different parts of Tomorrowland. The tram was dragging me from one place to another, in that world of dreams, the place that Walt Disney inaugurated as the "Happiest Place on Earth": a fountain of fun, happiness, and illusion for millions of children and adults coming from all corners of the planet. No one could hear very well. The speakers were describing inventions and historic moments. I was sitting next to my son and facing my daughter. My father-in-law was sitting diagonally from me. The phone rang. I didn't hear it, but I felt it vibrate. I saw the call was coming from *unknown*. I knew it was somebody calling from outside the U.S.: Lisa or my brother. It was my brother. He was boarding his flight to Madrid. From there he would fly directly to Buenos Aires. He'd also found an earlier flight. But he wouldn't see him. Neither would I. He calculated with better foresight than I. He knew it from the last time he was in the hospital. I didn't. I thought six months, a year, then two months, two weeks, one week. I read the messages without reading them, without assimilating the words. I had spoken with him the day before. I told him that I would come visit him, and he told me: "No! Why? Don't bother." I didn't tell him anything. I didn't answer. I changed my ticket for Tuesday. Tuesday??? My father was gone on Thursday, the day after we talked, in twenty-four hours, 1,440 minutes, 86,400 seconds. She writes: When my brother called me, I began to cry, and I couldn't stop. My father-in-law sat next to me to console me while my kids were crying, upset by seeing me like that. They didn't understand what was happening. In the "Happiest Place on Earth," while the tram I was on was twisting from one side to another, I got the news of my father's death.

Day No Number

Was it Vera who left for Buenos Aires and arrived late for the wake and the funeral? It had to be Gisela, since only she, that hybrid into which she had been transformed, would have left her passport in a drawer in her office. Vera would have brought it in her purse. She would have left directly from the Orlando International Airport. She didn't want to think about her father's body. She only imagined one more time, before he passed, that she held his hand tightly and caressed it. She looked into the depths of his sky-blue eyes and told him about her move, her work, how her kids were asking about him, and how her daughter took care of Mima, the teddy bear he had given her and whose belly had already been sewn up with pink thread so you couldn't see the seam. She thought about his eyes, wide open and sweet, looking at her patiently, smiling; two attentive eyes that followed her closely, at night, luminous, radiating in the darkness so she could see him, despite being on the other side, in an open space where he moved lightly and brilliantly, like a paper kite in a picture painted by an unknown artist.

# Biographical Information

**Gisela Heffes** is a professor of Latin American literature and culture at Johns Hopkins University. She is also a writer, ecocritic, and public intellectual with a particular focus on literature, media, and the environment. She is the author of several novels, including *Ischia* (Deep Vellum, 2023). She currently resides in Silver Spring, Maryland.

**Grady C. Wray** has taught Latin American literature, Spanish, and translation at The University of Oklahoma for over two decades. He published the first bilingual critical edition of Sor Juana Inés de la Cruz's *Devotional Exercises*. Apart from his critical work on women writers of the premodern period, his translations of poetry and fiction include *Ischia* (Deep Vellum, 2023) and *The Mobile Zero of Its Mouth* (katakana editores, 2020) by Gisela Heffes; *2323 Stratford Ave.* (Valparaiso Editions USA, 2018) by Marcelo Rioseco; and *Series 201* (*Latin American Literature Today*, 2017) by Luisa Valenzuela.